Why didn't she answ

Blake redialed Heidi's phor
voice mail.

She and his daughter were probably headed back, so he decided to meet them. He didn't have much time left with Heidi; he wouldn't waste a minute. But when he reached the creek, they weren't there, and a vague unease settled in his gut. He quickened his pace through the forest toward his house.

"Heidi! Maggie!"

No reason to panic. Heidi knew this mountain as well as he did.

But the house was empty. So was her cabin. Now his breath came in gasps as he tried her phone again. He left a message. "Heidi, where are you? Call me."

He ran down to the road, calling their names. But Heidi wouldn't allow Maggie to walk along the narrow road.

Blake rubbed his temples and tried to breathe. Tried to stop the thoughts from tumbling in his brain. Missing... Why?

Who?

His phone rang and his heart soared, then crashed when an unknown number lit up the screen. "Yes?"

"Hello, Blake," a cold voice said.

"Who is this?"

"I'm the person who has what you love most in the world."

Lynn Huggins Blackburn believes in the power of stories, especially those that remind us that true love exists, a gift from the Truest Love. She's passionate about CrossFit, coffee and chocolate (don't make her choose) and experimenting with recipes that feed both body and soul. She lives in South Carolina with her true love, Brian, and their three children. You can follow her real-life happily-ever-after at lynnhugginsblackburn.com.

Books by Lynn Huggins Blackburn

Love Inspired Suspense

Covert Justice

COVERT JUSTICE

LYNN HUGGINS BLACKBURN

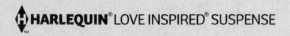

Recycling programs
for this product may
not exist in your area.

LOVE INSPIRED BOOKS

ISBN-13: 978-0-373-44677-3

Covert Justice

Copyright © 2015 by Lynn Huggins Blackburn

For God hath not given us the spirit of fear;
but of power, and of love, and of a sound mind.
–2 Timothy 1:7

To Brian. This book wouldn't exist without your encouragement and support. Thank you for believing in me, even—especially—when I thought this dream would never come true. I love you more!

Acknowledgments

So many people to thank!

My Savior—for everything.

My children—Emma, James and Drew—for making the real world a place I love to be.

My parents, Ken and Susan Huggins—for all those trips to the library, for encouraging my love of books and instilling in me the confidence to fly.

My sister, Jennifer Huggins Bayne—for loving the first words of the first story and loving me even when writing makes me crazy.

My mother-in-law, Sandra Blackburn—for your support and all those hours babysitting while I write.

Edie Melson and Vonda Skelton—for first welcoming me into the writing world.

Lissa Halls Johnson—for guiding me through the first version of this story.

The Light Brigade—for praying me through this amazing experience.

Lynette Eason—for telling me my first chapter was too slow and then helping me fix it. You're an awesome mentor!

Tamela Hancock Murray—for believing in my writing.

Elizabeth Mazer—for taking a chance on this story and this writer.

ONE

Blake Harrison pulled the hood of his jacket over his head and sprinted through the deluge. Nothing like a cold November downpour to cap off an exhausting week.

He slid into the seat of his BMW and pushed the hood away from his face. Dealing with multiple off-quality batches had kept him late every night this week.

If they didn't get a handle on their production issues soon, they ran a serious risk of missing shipments and losing customers. Losing customers meant losing jobs and Harrison Plastics International hadn't laid off an employee in sixty-three years. He didn't want to be the first Harrison in three generations to break faith with their employees. Their friends.

He shook off the gloominess. They'd had issues before and had overcome them without having to resort to personnel cuts. He had confidence in his engineering team. They'd get things working again. He'd be able to relax after he had a decent meal, a story time with his little Maggiemoo and a full eight-hour visit with his pillow.

He pulled out of the HPI parking lot and began the halfmile drive to his home. The rain made it hard to see the lines on the pavement and he kept his speed low as he entered the sharp curve marking the halfway point to his driveway.

Headlights coming up way too fast flashed in his rear-view mirror. Didn't that guy have the good sense to slow down? At least he wouldn't have to deal with him on his tail for long.

Without warning, the headlights grew larger in his mirror and a sudden impact threw him forward before the seat belt slammed him back into his seat. He tried to steer as the BMW skidded across the road but lost control on the wet pavement and crashed into the opposite ditch, tail-first.

He didn't know how long he sat there, hands clenched around the wheel. As his breathing slowed, he took a quick inventory. He could move his arms and legs. His neck and back would be killing him tomorrow, but he didn't think he'd suffered any major damage. He breathed a prayer of thanksgiving as he groped around in the seat for his cell phone to call for a tow truck.

Before he could find it, the passenger-side door flew open. He blinked in the brightness from the dome lights and tried to focus on the dark shape leaning into his car. He caught a glimpse of big green eyes filled with concern before a slender finger stretched out and extinguished the light.

"Can you move?" He could barely make out the words over the pounding rain. A small hand gripped his arm. "Blake? You have to focus."

What on earth?

She moved closer and unbuckled his seat belt. "Can you move?"

"Yes. What are you—"

"Then move!" She reached around the steering wheel, pushed open the driver's-side door and shoved him out into the downpour. He slipped on the bank and had just gotten his footing when she grabbed his hand. "Let's go. We have to get out of here."

"Hey." He shook her off. "I'm not going anywhere with you. I don't know you. I have to find my phone and—"

"Do you have a death wish?"

"What?"

"They're turning around. We have to get away from the car."

Turning around? The meaning of her words soaked in. They'd hit him on purpose?

"This way." When her hand clasped his, he allowed her to pull him away from the wreckage and up the bank. As they dove into the trees, headlights flashed around the curve and the air filled with the unmistakable sound of metal dragging across asphalt.

He turned and watched in horror as a massive truck sped away from the mangled remains of his car.

"—close." The mystery woman had her phone to her ear. "Send an ambulance."

"I don't need an ambulance," he said. "I need answers." Why would anyone do this? He didn't have any enemies. Well, a few, but none that would run him off the road and try to kill him. "Who are you?"

The sound of sirens pierced the air and she backed away. "Who I am doesn't matter. In fact, it would be best if you don't mention me to the authorities at all."

She disappeared into the woods faster than he would have thought possible. He could try to follow her, but in the dark and rain, he wouldn't have a clue which direction she'd gone. He stared at the spot where she'd disappeared and called out, "Thank you," before sliding back down the bank as the first police car pulled to the side, lights flashing blue and eerie in the gloom.

The next few hours passed in a haze of images. Police and ambulance lights illuminating the surrounding forest. The officer telling him an anonymous caller had reported the accident. His dad standing beside the remains of the car, shaking his head in disbelief. The smell of gasoline mixed with the scent of torn earth. The EMTs insisting he ride to the hospital in the ambulance. His sister, Caroline, clad in hot pink rain boots and jacket, tears streaming down her face when she saw him in the emergency room. His mother's relieved voice when he spoke to her and his daughter, Maggie, assuring them he'd be home soon.

One CT scan and several exams later, they released him as Saturday dawned clear and cool. Caroline drove with extra caution, for her, and took him straight to their parents' home to pick up Maggie. Through it all, not one person suggested he'd been the victim of an attempted murder. The police were treating it as a hit-and-run. Given his minimal injuries, and knowing he carried plenty of car insurance, he doubted the investigation would go far.

He didn't know why he hadn't mentioned the mystery woman's involvement. Not even to his dad. There had never seemed to be a good time to bring it up.

But she'd been there. She'd appeared out of nowhere, jumped into his car and pushed him to safety, risking her own life in the process. And somehow she'd known his attacker would turn around to try again.

Which left him with two burning questions.

When the driver, whoever they were, found out he had survived, what then?

And who was she?

FBI Special Agent Heidi Zimmerman pulled through a fast-food drive-through minutes before they stopped serving breakfast. She'd spent the night at the hospital keeping an eye on the Harrisons while a tactical operations crew worked in the rain to install surveillance equipment at all three of the Harrisons' homes.

No one ran surveillance like TacOps, but the parameters of her mission hadn't included keeping tabs on the Harrisons.

Until now.

When she'd called the agent in charge of the TacOps team, Special Agent Kyle Richards, and explained what had happened, he'd offered to expand their surveillance parameters to include the Harrisons.

If anyone decided to sneak around on their property, the TacOps guys would let her know.

She sat at the small desk in her hotel room and spread out her breakfast. She'd taken one bite when the phone rang.

"What on earth were you thinking?" Special Agent in Charge, Frank Cunningham, her boss and godfather, sounded like he wanted to strangle her.

"You'd rather I'd sat back and let someone kill him?"

"You went in there with no backup—"

"I called Max."

" —blew your cover—"

"Blake Harrison's the only one who saw."

"—could have been killed—"

"Like that isn't an everyday occurrence."

"—and defied a direct order."

Someone else spoke, but she couldn't catch the words. Uncle Frank sighed. "Jacobs is defending you. Says he'd have done the same thing."

"I said I hope I would have," her partner, Max Jacobs, said. He must have stepped closer to the speaker. "Are you okay?" In spite of her frustration, Heidi smiled. Max was the brother she'd never had. She had no doubt he'd chew her out later, but just like most siblings, he wouldn't sit back and let anyone else rip into her. Whenever she was under fire, he always, always had her back.

"Need some sleep." She yawned. "Otherwise, I'm fine."

"And Blake Harrison?"

"No concussion or broken bones. Wouldn't be surprised to learn he has whiplash."

"Beats the alternative."

No doubt.

"Who saw you?" Uncle Frank's tone hadn't softened.

"No one."

"They didn't notice your car?"

"Give me some credit." Uncle Frank's skills included knowing how to push every button she had. He wouldn't talk to his other agents this way. No. He reserved this level of tough love for her and her alone. "I left it in an overgrown abandoned driveway. That rain was no joke. You could barely see the road, much less a car hidden in the brush twenty feet off the pavement. No one saw me leave, either."

"Can you identify the car?"

"Truck. Full-size. Dark. Plates covered in dirt. Matches the description of half the trucks in the county. Should have some paint transfer, but my guess is they'll wipe it down and ditch it. And I doubt they bought it legally in the first place."

"We'll check for stolen trucks in the area," Max said. "Maybe we'll get a hit."

She appreciated the effort Max was making to diffuse the tension.

"Can you explain to me what you were doing there in the first place? Or why on earth someone tried to kill Blake Harrison?"

Heidi snapped. "I don't have a clue why someone tried to kill him, Uncle Frank. Maybe he's got more enemies than we knew about. I'll be sure to ask him." Did he expect her to solve the case before she even started the job? "As for what I was doing there, I believe it's called running surveillance. It's what I do when I go undercover. I'm pretty sure it's what you taught me to do."

Uncle Frank didn't respond.

"I was sitting at the edge of the parking lot and I saw a

car leave at an odd time. The shift didn't end for another hour. I thought I'd have time to follow the driver to see if they did anything suspicious and be back by the end of the shift. My plan had been to see if anyone hung around late on a Friday."

"Good idea, Z." Bless Max.

"The rain was so heavy, I didn't realize it was Blake Harrison until I'd already pulled in behind him. He turned onto the road and I almost let him go, but this truck came up fast and…"

"And what?"

"And I don't know why I followed them. I just did."

"She's got the best instincts of any agent I've ever worked with," Max said. "They've saved my life more than once."

"I guess it's good for Blake Harrison that you followed your gut," Uncle Frank finally conceded.

Heidi knew that was as close as she was going to get to an apology.

"You're going to have to read him in. Soon. He needs to know who he can and cannot talk to about this." At least Uncle Frank's voice had returned to normal decibels.

"I'll take care of it."

"Great," Max said with enough brightness to rival a high school cheerleader. "Z, you need to get some rest. We'll let you know if we learn anything on the truck."

"Heidi, remember what you promised me." Uncle Frank's words erased all her frustration with him. His anger wasn't directed at her. His anger reflected his fear for her safety.

"I'll be careful."

She ended the call, finished her breakfast and took a long shower before falling across the bed. She'd found the cheap mattress hard for the past month, but today it didn't matter.

The ringing phone jolted her back to consciousness. The clock on the bedside table read five-thirty. She'd slept seven hours?

"Hello." She stretched and cleared her throat.

"Did I wake you?" Max laughed.

"No."

"Liar."

"What do you want?" Heidi sat up and scanned the room. Satisfied she was alone, she leaned back onto the pillows.

"First, Sara would like you to know that if you ever do something that stupid again, she will no longer be your best friend."

"Sara's survived worse. I'm not worried."

"Well, she is."

"How does she even know about this?" Sara had been her best friend since the first night in their freshman college dorm. When she'd woken up screaming, she'd expected Sara to bolt. She wouldn't have blamed her.

Instead, Sara had stayed. She'd kept Heidi's secrets. She'd taught Heidi how to laugh again. And she'd made no secret that having a roommate with a traumatic past had led to her decision to make PTSD her specialty. She was now Dr. Sara Elliot, a practicing clinical psychologist who consulted frequently with the FBI, CIA and other law enforcement and intelligence agencies. Her security clearance was even higher than Uncle Frank's.

Heidi had never understood why Sara and Max weren't on better terms. It would make her life a lot easier if her two best friends could get along but she seemed to be the only thing they could agree on.

"She came in to see Frank about fifteen minutes after he hung up with you. He's the one who ratted you out. Not me."

"Well, good. That will save me some time the next time I talk to her."

"Seriously, Z. We're all concerned about you. The Kovacs don't play." Max wasn't laughing anymore.

"I know that better than anyone."

Max didn't respond.

Heidi let him stew for a minute. He was worried. Sara was worried. Uncle Frank was worried. She appreciated the concern, but there was no way she'd pass up the chance to take down the Kovacs. She'd never been this close before.

"Did you have a reason for waking me up other than to fuss at me?"

"I called because I thought you might like to know a forest ranger found a burned-out Ford F-150 in the Pisgah National Forest, next county over. Matches a vehicle reported stolen on Wednesday."

"Okay."

"Z?"

"Yeah."

"I'm not sure this is going to be as straightforward as we'd hoped."

"It never is."

"You need to find out what Blake Harrison has done to tick off the Kovac family."

"I don't think he has any idea."

"What makes you say that?"

"The look on his face last night. He wasn't expecting to be run down on a rainy highway and he never imagined they'd done it on purpose. I spent the entire evening watching the family at the hospital. The dad, Jeffrey, and the sister, Caroline, were worried, but they weren't scared."

"They should be."

"They will be."

"Have you thought about how you're going to handle letting him know what's going on?"

"I'm hoping to catch him alone. TacOps is monitoring the place."

"No small job."

"Tell me about it."

The Harrisons owned a huge swath of property. The land had been in the family for over a hundred years. The family business, Harrison Plastics International, known by everyone in the area as HPI, sat on one side of the road in the valley between two small mountains. One mountain was undeveloped and used as a recreation area for the employees of HPI. The Harrisons' homes dotted the small mountain on the other side.

Blake's home sat on the backside of the mountain, while his parents' home sat in the middle overlooking the valley and the plant. Caroline's home perched near the top of the mountain above their parents'. A gate blocked the winding driveway leading to their houses, but it wouldn't stop anyone determined to get inside.

"Richards is leading the TacOps team," Heidi continued.

"Good man."

"He's supposed to let me know if there's a good opportunity to pay Blake Harrison a visit. If nothing comes up soon, I may just have to knock on his door."

TWO

It was 7:28 p.m. Blake swallowed three more ibuprofen. They'd offered him a prescription for stronger pain medication before releasing him from the hospital. He'd refused. He'd seen firsthand how far prescription drugs could take someone and he didn't want that stuff in his house again.

He tried to bend over to pull Maggie's doll from under the couch, but his back had other ideas. The rap on the door caught him off guard and he jerked upright. Pain raced through his sore muscles as he reached for the baseball bat he'd unearthed when he'd returned home this morning.

Someone had tried to kill him last night. Not that anyone knew, but when his ex-wife's parents had offered to take Maggie for the evening, he'd jumped at it. At age five, Maggie's response to the idea of him being injured was to climb all over him to make sure he was in one piece. His aching back could use a night off from being her jungle gym. And anyway, she had to be safer with her grandparents than with him.

Wait. What if they'd tapped his phone? They could have been listening and that would mean they knew he was alone. If he looked through the peephole, would they shoot him?

Get a grip, man. He'd watched too many movies.

The knock came again.

"Mr. Harrison?"

He knew that voice.

He risked a peek and got an eyeful of curly bronze hair. She stepped back from the door as he tried to match this woman with the version he had in his head. Hair saturated with rain, plastered to her cheeks. Eyes flashing. A bit on the bossy side, not that he would complain.

"Mr. Harrison?"

The voice. Yes. He would know her voice anywhere. Although last night she'd called him Blake. He preferred Blake. He opened the door before he could change his mind.

"Hi."

Yes, same eyes, flashing with amusement now as she studied him.

He followed her gaze to the bat clenched in his hand. He considered putting it down, but really, what did he know about her?

Besides the fact that she'd saved his life.

"May I come in?"

He hesitated and looked behind her. A small Acura SUV sat in his driveway. "How did you get in here?"

"Your code's not complicated."

His mind raced with the implications. She knew where he lived. She'd had no difficulty entering their gated driveway. She hadn't tried to hide either of those facts.

"Mr. Harrison?"

He met her gaze.

"I'd rather not stand on your porch all evening. If you don't want me to come in, I'd be happy to meet you somewhere more public."

"No." No way could he let her get away without giving him some kind of explanation for what was going on. Although he doubted he'd be able to stop her if she wanted to leave.

He stuck out his hand. "My name is Blake Harrison."

She grinned as she shook it. "Pleased to meet you, Mr. Harrison. I'm Heidi Zimmerman."

"It's nice to meet you. Please come in. And please, call me Blake." He opened the door wider and stepped to the side. "Have a seat."

He didn't miss the way her eyes darted around the room as she crossed the threshold, or the way she chose a chair with a view of the door and the rest of the room.

"Thank you," she said. "How are you feeling?"

"Fine." Her smirk told him she wasn't buying it. "I'm moving slow, but there's no permanent damage. Thanks to you."

They stared at each other for a moment. He got the impression that she was analyzing everything he said, every move he made, but he couldn't be sure what she'd concluded about him. "Can I offer you a Coke? Mountain Dew? Tea? Water?"

"Water would be great."

He tried not to let on how stiff he was as he walked to the kitchen.

Her voice followed him. "You have a lovely home."

"Thanks. It was my grandparents'. I inherited it after they passed away."

Why on earth had he said that? He grabbed a water for her and a Mountain Dew for himself. Returning to the living room, he handed her the bottle and eased into the chair across from her. He had so many questions, but no idea where to start.

She reached into the back pocket of her jeans and removed a small leather case. She flipped it open and slid it across the coffee table. "Maybe this will help."

He read the words on the badge. FBI? Was this for real?

"Need a closer look? You can call headquarters, if you'd like to verify it's legitimate."

FBI? A lead weight settled on his chest as the faint hope

that the events of last night were a fluke disintegrated. "I think I'd like to hear what you have to say first."

"Fair enough," she said. "I need you to know, before last night I had no idea you were in danger."

The way she looked at him with her head cocked to the side, brows knit, mouth tight, he couldn't question the sincerity or concern behind her words.

Then again, for all he knew the FBI gave their agents acting classes.

He'd fallen for a pretty face once before. And Heidi Zimmerman qualified as more than a pretty face. Her hair spiraled past her shoulders in shades of blond and brown and one little curl kept breaking free from where she tucked it behind her ear. Long lashes framed big green eyes set over a cute nose.

Cute nose? Nobody had a cute nose. He needed to pull it together. What had she said? She hadn't known someone wanted him dead? What did someone say to that? Great?

She sat straighter in her chair. "I'm sure this goes without saying, but if you tell anyone what I'm about to tell you, I'll deny it and you'll be prosecuted for obstruction of justice."

"Sounds fun."

Her lips twitched. Super FBI agent lady had a sense of humor. Interesting.

No trace of humor lingered when she spoke again. "Fifty years ago, Viktor Kovac immigrated to America from Hungary. It didn't take him long to settle into New York City and within a few years, more members of the family joined him. Within ten years of his arrival, the Kovacs had made a name for themselves in criminal circles. The police suspected them of everything from money laundering to drug smuggling."

She took a sip of her water. "Like most organized crime families, they are focused on doing whatever it takes to protect their own and make as much money as they can. In recent years the younger Kovacs have pushed into darker territory. Instead of money laundering and protection schemes, they've been linked to human trafficking, arms smuggling and trying to corner the market on certain prescription drugs."

"I've never heard of them."

"No. You wouldn't. Other than the occasional low-ranking lieutenant or wannabe, they've never been prosecuted."

"Never?"

She shook her head, disgust etching her features. "They've been linked to multiple homicides yet despite extraordinary efforts on the part of detectives, FBI agents and even informants, there's never been enough proof to take them to trial, much less secure a conviction."

Her voice cracked and for a moment, a cavern of pain opened in her eyes. As quickly as it appeared, she looked away and when their eyes met again, steely determination was in its place.

"The younger Kovacs are opportunists. They function without morals, ethics or loyalty to anything or anyone other than the family."

"You don't have to convince me. They're bad news. I'll be sure to stay away from them."

"I'm afraid that won't be as easy as you may think."

"What are you talking about? I don't know any Kovacs."

When she looked at him her eyes filled, not with the intensity he'd seen a moment ago, but with compassion. She had the look his mother had had when she'd told him about Grandma's cancer. A look like that only came with bad news.

"Are you saying I *do* know some Kovacs?"

She nodded. "One of your employees."

"I know all my employees. Not a Kovac in the bunch."

"Two months ago, you hired a man by the name of Mark Hammond, I believe?"

"Yes."

"Mark Hammond isn't his real name."

Blake put his head in his hands. This couldn't be happening. "I run background checks on all my employees."

"If you've got the money and the know-how, it's not hard to create an identity that can withstand all but the most thorough of investigations."

"So—"

"Mark Hammond's real name is Markos Kovac. He's the youngest grandson of the original Kovac and he has a lot to prove. He's the baby of the family by quite a few years and most of his older brothers have already established their roles in the organization."

Blake sat up. "How do you know this?"

"The Kovac family is my job."

She didn't elaborate and the set of her mouth made him think she might not say more, but she swallowed hard and continued. "I know more about the Kovacs than anyone else in the Bureau. When Markos and his wife, Katarina, bolted for North Carolina, I followed. I've been here four weeks, watching, following, listening—trying to figure out what Markos is up to."

"I haven't seen you."

"I'm an undercover agent. That's kind of the idea."

Something about this whole conversation didn't make sense. "What does any of this have to do with me? Mark may not like me, but I don't think he'd run me off the road. Besides, I hate to tell you this, but he was at work when I left."

She started to answer, but he cut her off. "Has it occurred to you that maybe this guy wants to go straight? Maybe he wants to get out of the family business and live an honest life."

She bit the inside of her lip. "No one leaves the Kovacs. No one has even tried in the past fifteen years." The words were more breath than whisper. She looked up at him and the pain on her face made him lean toward her. He wanted to comfort her, somehow, but he didn't even know her.

The moment passed. "What do you mean, about Markos not liking you?"

Blake rubbed his face with his hands. "I'm sure it's nothing. We've just had a few minor issues."

"If it's all the same to you, I'd like to decide whether your issues are minor or not."

Ah. Yes. There was the bossiness he remembered. "Fine. He's had some inconsistencies with quality that none of our other supervisors have had. The last twenty or so off-quality batches we've produced happened on his watch. I've questioned him, even hung out during shifts, tried to ask around. There's nothing I could prove in terms of negligence in his work, but I did tell Dad and Caroline that I was watching him. We've been wondering if he might be some sort of corporate spy."

"Do you have a lot of trouble with corporate espionage?"

Blake couldn't resist the opportunity to brag. "We make things no one else can make. Sure, we produce a lot of stuff that's standard—your basic water bottles, food containers, chemical containers—but over the past ten years, we've built a reputation for making specialty containers no one else will even attempt. We make unique shapes and if we can't make it, no one can. This year we landed a huge account for water bottles shaped like footballs, basketballs and baseballs. Our client has already sold them to over thirty professional teams. They hit baseball parks this summer. That account alone doubled the production on our specialty lines."

She didn't seem as impressed as she should be.

"We have some fierce competitors out there who would love to get an inside look at what we do."

Heidi raised her hands. "Okay. Okay. You guys are the best. I'm not disputing your status. But I know the Kovacs, and corporate espionage isn't their style," she said. "He's here to do more than steal some trade secrets."

"Care to be more specific?"

Heidi looked down. "I can't."

"You what?"

"I can't be more specific, because I don't know. That's what I'm here to find out."

Blake sat back in his chair. Heidi watched as the struggle to grasp her words played out across his face. They sat in silence for several minutes before he cleared his throat. "What does any of this have to do with me getting run off the road last night?"

There it was. The question she'd been waiting for and the one she dreaded answering. "I don't know. I'm hoping you might be able to help with that."

Skepticism radiated from his face. "Me?"

"One of the things that has bugged me from the beginning is why Markos chose HPI."

"I'm not sure I'm following you."

"You make plastic containers. What's dangerous about plastic? Sure, you store chemicals in high quantity, but he'd be able to get those in other places—places run by men who don't have your reputation for high moral standards. I can't figure out the connection between what you do at HPI and what he could be planning. But after last night, I'm certain of one thing."

"What?"

"He believes you are standing in his way."

Blake stood and paced around the small living room. He'd taken this far better than she'd expected. He hadn't thrown anything. He hadn't asked her to leave. He hadn't refused to believe her. His mind had to be in turmoil, but he didn't appear rattled. If anything, he looked like a man who was formulating a plan of action.

No. Not what she'd expected at all.

He turned to her. "Are you hungry?"

"Hungry?"

"Yes. I'm starving. How do you feel about pizza?"

"My feelings are generally favorable toward anything that involves cheese."

A true smile flickered across his face and Heidi looked at him, really looked at him, for the first time. Dark hair with a hint of curl. Dark brown eyes. Strong chin. He reminded her of the brooding movie stars of the '40s. Until he smiled. His smile did something funny to her, but she didn't have the time or inclination to explore the emotion.

He pondered the phone in his hand. "Is it safe for me to have a pizza delivered?"

She could tell he was trying to keep things light, even as he processed the seriousness of the situation. "It should be, but to be sure, you can use my phone."

He took her phone and dialed the number from memory. "What do you like?"

"Meat. The more the better."

He widened his eyes at her. "I'd have taken you for a vegetarian."

"I'd starve."

He placed the order and returned her phone before settling back into his chair. He grimaced as he sat. He had to be hurting.

He pulled in a deep breath and winced again. He could use the accident as a cop-out. He could tell her he didn't feel well and needed to get some rest. Most people would.

Not Blake Harrison. "I want to talk more about this situation, but first, I need to know more about you."

Heidi wasn't sure where he was going with this, but it was a fair question. "Okay. What do you want to know?"

"Who are you?" Frustration oozed from his words. She needed to remember he'd had less than thirty minutes to come to terms with some life-altering news.

"My name is Heidi Zimmerman. I'm an FBI agent and

for the past ten years, the Kovac family has been my primary assignment."

"Ten years? How old are you?"

"It's none of your business, but I'm thirty-two. I joined the Bureau straight out of college. Virginia Tech. I have a degree in mechanical engineering and a minor in accounting."

"Interesting combination."

"The Kovacs own several manufacturing enterprises. I've gone undercover as an engineer more than once."

"How'd you wind up with the FBI?"

Heidi gave him the answer she gave to anyone who asked. "I was always interested in law enforcement. Seemed exciting and fulfilling. So I went for it."

Blake studied her, then shook his head. "I've believed pretty much everything you've said, but I don't think that's the real reason."

Heidi froze. How could he—?

"If you don't want to tell me, fine. Spare me the slick story that could be an advertisement for the FBI recruiters to use. It doesn't suit you."

Heidi didn't answer right away. She hadn't expected Blake Harrison to be so perceptive. But the truth? The truth wasn't something she shared. Ever. She couldn't. Not if she wanted to live to fight another day.

"I didn't lie," she said. Blake started to argue with her but she cut him off. "I grew up rough. There were a few police officers who made a huge impact on me. Then this FBI agent saved my life." She'd skated into dangerous territory and decided to keep it vague. "By the time I graduated from high school, I had my heart set on joining the FBI, but with my background, I didn't know if the FBI would take me. I chose college courses so I could work in something other than law enforcement if plan A didn't pan out."

She hadn't come anywhere close to telling him the whole

truth, but not one word of what she'd said was a lie. She gave him time to process her words.

"Why are you embarrassed about your childhood?" he finally asked.

How had he made that leap? And how annoying that he was right. "Look, not everyone has a Norman Rockwell up-bringing. Mine isn't something I talk about. When people ask, I give them the recruiting-poster version. It's cleaner. And most people don't like messy."

He nodded. "That I believe. But you shouldn't assume my life has been all sunshine and roses."

No. She knew about that. She'd had background checks run on the entire Harrison family. Not because they were suspects, but more than one operation had gone south because an agent hadn't done their homework.

The Harrisons had checked out. An American success story. Family-owned business, strong family, loyal employees.

Except for one.

Blake closed his eyes and shook his head. "You know about Lana, don't you?"

She wouldn't deny it.

"Do I even want to know how you know?"

"Background checks are a standard part of an operation like this." His eyes flashed and Heidi pressed on. Might as well rip the bandage off in one quick pull. "As soon as Markos got the job, I ran background checks and financials on your entire family. Even pulled some reports on your grandparents, looking for any connection to the Kovacs, however slight. I didn't find anything that raised any red flags."

"Except Lana."

"Her, um, mistakes, were a matter of public record. As was your divorce and her relinquishment of her parental rights while in prison."

Blake fidgeted in his chair. Frustration? Embarrassment? Or trying to find a more comfortable position? Heidi couldn't be sure.

Heidi's phone buzzed in her pocket. She silenced it without looking. As a rule, she kept her phone out of sight when she was meeting with someone on official business. If she was going to ask them to trust her, they deserved to get her undivided attention.

The phone vibrated again. Two calls in ten seconds? It might be time to break her rule.

Blake waved his Mountain Dew toward her. "Seems like someone wants to talk to you. Go ahead."

"Sorry about this." She caught the call before it went to voice mail. "Zimmerman."

"Are you still with Blake Harrison?"

Max? "Yes."

"Stay with him." Max's tone left no doubt. Something bad had happened.

"What—"

"Hang on."

Blake's phone rang and his brow furrowed as he glanced at it. She waved a hand to encourage him to take it.

"Mom? Mom, slow down. What—"

His face registered confusion, then concern, then horror. "I'll be right there. Call me if anything changes. Tell Dad I love him. Yes. I love you, too."

He dropped his phone on the table. "They're taking Dad to the hospital in Asheville. Mom thinks he's had a stroke." He stood and rummaged around in a basket on the kitchen counter. "I have keys to Mom's car in here somewhere."

A stroke? This explained the call from Max.

Max came back on the line. "Heidi," Max said.

"I know. Stroke?"

"Maybe. Maybe not. Don't let Blake Harrison out of your sight."

THREE

Heidi slid her phone into her bag, retrieved her keys and stepped into the kitchen where Blake pawed through the small basket.

"Good grief." He dumped the basket on the counter. "Where are they?"

"Blake." If he heard her, he didn't acknowledge her. She put one hand over his. That got his attention.

"Look, I'm sorry," he said. "I have to go."

She jangled her keys. "I know. I'll drive."

He froze. "What?"

"I'm coming with you."

"Why?"

Bless his heart. He didn't understand. "Blake, someone tried to kill you last night. You have the grandson of a notorious organized-crime family working for you. Now your dad has a stroke?" He had to see the pattern here.

"My grandfather died from a stroke in his early sixties."

"Then this may be nothing more than a horrible coincidence, but I'm not willing to take that chance. Let me drive."

They loaded into her car with no further conversation. She didn't need his occasional prompts to turn left or right, but this probably wasn't the best time to tell him that she'd already made it a point to know how to get to the nearest hospitals.

He stared out the window as she drove and she didn't try to interrupt his thoughts. She'd unloaded a lot of information on him. He had to be exhausted from the long night in the hospital, and now this.

When her phone rang, she answered, aware that his face had paled. She held the phone to her ear, rather than letting the audio play through the car's Bluetooth system.

"Zimmerman."

"Just talked to Richards," Max said. "They have eyes on the little girl. She's watching a movie. Both grandparents in the house. No suspicious activity. Team's prepared to stay all night."

"Good."

"Caroline Harrison's phone indicates she's heading to Asheville."

As expected.

"Kovac is at home."

"Are we sure?"

"Yes. He's sitting on his back porch smoking. TacOps says he's been out there for thirty minutes and he's been home all day."

"So…"

"We'll keep an eye on things. We'll get some blood samples and have our guys run tests for anything suspicious."

She could feel Blake's eyes boring into her and chose her words with care. "I would think it would be difficult to cause a stroke without there being other warning signs."

Anyone who'd ever watched a crime drama or a spy thriller would know certain drugs and poisons could be used to induce a heart attack, but a stroke?

"It should be," Max said. "I have a call in to a few of our bioterrorism experts to be sure there isn't something new out there we haven't heard of. The only drugs or poisons I know that can cause a stroke would have to be consumed in such high quantities that they'd have to be administered over time, with a gradual buildup of symptoms. He should have been too sick to be sitting around having dinner one minute and then be exhibiting full-on stroke symptoms the next."

"Unless someone's found a way to induce a stroke that looks like a natural one."

"Exactly."

"Let me know what they say."

"I will. You okay?"

"Yeah. Should be at the hospital in fifteen minutes."

"Okay. Tell Blake the latest is his dad's stable. They've administered those stroke drugs. He's breathing on his own and talking to the docs."

"I will."

"Z. Be careful."

"I will."

She hit End and glanced at Blake. "Your dad is stable and talking to the doctors."

He blinked in surprise. "Do I want to know how you know that?"

"If you don't, then you aren't going to like the rest of it." She filled him in on Caroline's location and Maggie's.

"How on earth do you know all this?"

"While you were in the hospital last night, a judge gave us permission to put traces on your phones. And we set up some passive surveillance at your homes and your in-laws' home, since you and Maggie are there so often. Some video feeds on the outside, motion sensors, stuff like that. We have no intention or desire to violate your privacy. This is all for your protection, I assure you. I didn't think you'd object."

"I don't know how I feel about that." Blake frowned. "We can discuss it later. Why do you think Maggie is in danger? Even if I'm somehow a problem for Mark's plan, what reason would he have to target my daughter?"

Heidi's mind flitted to that sunny afternoon fifteen years ago. The smells. The heat. The pain. No. Not again. She shook off the foreboding.

Blake needed to be concerned enough to work with them, to take the necessary precautions, but not so worried that he couldn't carry on business as usual. "I don't want to think she is, but I'm not willing to take any chances, because the truth is I can't guarantee we can keep anyone safe."

She let that hang there, not wanting to rush past it and have it look like she was trying to gloss over this harshest of realities. "We don't know why Kovac is here or what his end game is. We don't know if your family is at risk or not. Up until last night, we assumed you were safe and we were wrong. We've been tracking Kovac's movements, but now we have a system set up to alert us if he approaches any member of your family outside the plant walls. By tracking your phones and cars, we'll know if anyone decides to take off on an unplanned trip and we'll know if anyone's phone suddenly goes dead."

Blake shifted in his seat. "Don't take this the wrong way, but that's not much. Cell phones and locations are all well and good, but if somebody decides to kidnap my daughter or my mother—"

Heidi held up a hand. "We doubt either of them are targets, but we have systems in place to monitor their whereabouts. If anything looks suspicious, I'll be notified. After what happened last night, I've put in a request to get additional support at your home, but with your houses the way they are, it may be tricky."

She paused as she waited for the traffic to clear so she could turn left. "We're looking for a rental property close to the plant we can use as a base of operation."

He shook his head. "This is way past weird."

"I wish I could tell you it won't get weirder, but it will."

"Awesome." Blake rubbed his hands over his face.

They rode in silence for a few minutes before Heidi risked a question. "I was going to ask you this before your mom called. Do you work late often?"

"You don't already know?"

The words held a mixture of hostility and teasing that made it impossible for her to be angry with him. "No. Your family has been on the periphery of my surveillance. Not the main focus."

"Okay. That makes sense, but I don't understand what my work schedule has to do with anything."

"I'm trying to get a handle on how difficult it would have been for him to plan the attack against you last night."

He adjusted the seat belt at his neck. "I almost never work late."

That didn't fit with the profile she'd been building in her head.

"I work hard while I'm there, and then leave by four-thirty unless I'm covering for one of the engineers or dealing with some major production issues. I make it a point to spend evenings with Maggie. I take her to Brazilian Jiu-Jitsu classes one afternoon a week, and she loves sports. We just finished soccer and are getting ready to start basketball. If we don't have practice or a game, then we hang out at home. If I have things I didn't get to during the day, I log in to the system from home and work after she goes to bed."

"So Kovac took advantage of a rare opportunity."

"If that's what you want to call it," he said.

She decided to take the conversation to a lighter topic. "How did you ever land on Brazilian Jiu-Jitsu?"

"I earned my black belt a few years ago and I want Maggie to be able to defend herself."

So much for a lighter topic.

They didn't talk the rest of the way. Heidi didn't mind silence, but most people she knew had to fill it with something. Blake Harrison didn't fit the mold of anyone she knew.

The security guards gave them a curt nod as they entered the hospital. Her weapons could pass for ordinary objects, but not having to submit to a bag search made things much easier.

She punched the up arrow on the elevator. "As long as you're here, pretend I don't exist."

"What?"

"There's no logical explanation for my presence, or for you to know who I am."

"Right."

"Hand me your phone."

"My what?"

"Your phone. I'll put my number in there. Then if you see anything suspicious, you can call or text."

He handed her the phone. She returned it as the elevator settled on the fifth floor.

"I'll be nearby. Leave whenever you're ready. I'll catch up in the parking lot."

When the elevator doors opened, Heidi stepped off without a backward glance. To anyone watching, they were two strangers on an elevator.

Except no one watching would know she'd saved his life. Or that she was an undercover FBI agent seeking to take down a notorious crime family. She wasn't kidding. The more he thought about it, the weirder this whole mess got.

He spotted Caroline and rushed to her side. "How's he doing?"

Caroline rocked back and forth on her heels. "Okay, I think."

His mom came out and he pulled her into a long hug.

"Your dad's waiting for you," she said. "They said you could both come back."

Blake followed his mom through the ICU. They passed the nurses' station and a break room where someone had burned popcorn. The stench was overpowering, but he pre-

ferred it to the antiseptic hospital smell permeating everything else.

His mom paused before a small room. "Your dad wants
to talk to each of you alone for a minute."

He shot a glance at Caroline, her eyes wide in fear. "Go
ahead, Care Bear." As much as he wanted to see his dad,
he had a feeling Caroline needed to see him, and hear what
he had to say, more.

His mom leaned against the wall and closed her eyes.
"This is not how I expected this day to go." He put an arm
around her and rested his cheek on her head while they
waited. He let his eyes travel around the ICU to see if he
noticed anything suspicious. Trouble was, he had no idea
what he was looking for. Maybe a janitor who lingered too
long in a room, or a visitor who didn't have the same look of
concern worn by the families of the patients in these walls?

His dad's stroke was probably due to heredity and not
foul play, but with his entire body aching from the events
of last night—had it only been twenty-four hours ago?—
he couldn't shake the fear gripping his heart.

Was Mark trying to eliminate the Harrison men or did he
have his eyes set on the entire family? Or was it just him?
What could they have done that would justify murder? Or
were they in the way of something he planned?

He scanned the room again, trying to be observant without being obvious about it. It was harder than it sounded
and he wished he knew where Heidi was.

More than anything, he wished no terror lurked in the
wings and that he'd never had a reason to meet her, in an
official capacity, but it was hard to dislike a woman who'd
saved his life. Or one who'd taken such a keen interest in
keeping his family safe.

Caroline came out of the room teary but smiling. "Your
turn," she said.

He stepped through the door, pausing in the dim light

to get his bearings and to be certain no one else was in the room before crossing to hug his dad.

His dad had always been his rock. The one thing that couldn't change. Seeing him lying on the white sheets, his face pale, a slight droop to one side of his mouth, was almost more than he could bear.

"Hey." His dad tried to smile. Half of his face cooperated. "It's going to be okay."

Blake swallowed. How would it ever be okay?

"There's a scary nurse that's going to come in here soon. Before she does, I want us to pray."

"What?"

"Let's pray."

Blake took his dad's hand and bowed his head.

"Father, You know how proud I am of my son. No father could be prouder. So I ask You now to comfort him. Ease his mind and his heart. Give him the strength to face the challenges of the days ahead. Give him the grace to trust You no matter what comes. Help him to remember that You are in control and nothing that has happened has caught You by surprise. In Jesus' name, I ask these things, Amen."

"Thanks, Dad," Blake said. His dad couldn't know how desperately he needed God to answer that prayer.

His time with his dad was cut short by the entrance of the nurse who didn't look as if she'd appreciate being asked to come back a few minutes later.

His mom met him at the door. "Go home. Get some rest."

"I hate to leave you alone."

"I'll be fine. I've told Caroline I want her to go home, too. I'll call you if anything changes." She placed one hand on his cheek like she'd done since he was a little boy. "He's going to recover, Blake, but we need you to be able to run things at the plant and you can't do that if you're worn out. You're going to have your hands full for a few weeks."

She had no idea.

FOUR

When he walked back into the waiting room, he tried not to stare in Heidi's direction. She was sitting in a corner. He assumed it was because that position gave her a good view of everyone entering and leaving and kept anyone from sneaking up on her from behind. She was holding something in her hands and as he got closer he realized what it was.

She was knitting.

Knitting?

Her fingers continued wrapping and circling and twisting yarn and she didn't appear to have noticed his arrival.

"You ready?" Caroline put the magazine she'd been skimming back on the stack and stretched a few times in her seat before standing.

"I guess." He looked back toward the ICU. "Seems wrong to leave, though."

Caroline laced her arm through his. "She'll need us to be able to relieve her tomorrow."

Blake stifled a yawn. He couldn't deny that his body craved sleep the way it craved Mountain Dew in the morning. But he couldn't shake the idea that this stroke might not have been a natural event. Someone might have done something to cause this. What if his dad was in great danger?

Who was he kidding? What could he do about it if he

was? Sure, he could protect himself if someone got close enough to throw a punch, but running him off the road? His dad having a stroke at dinner?

How could he protect his family from an enemy he couldn't see, couldn't touch and didn't understand?

For one brief moment he caught Heidi's eye. She nodded toward the elevator and her look conveyed the message that she thought he should leave. He found himself compelled to trust her and that frightened him almost as much as the mysterious Kovac family.

He knew better than to trust a stranger too soon.

Still…

Caroline propelled him toward the elevator. As they waited, he noticed Heidi had stopped knitting. With a few practiced moves, she rolled up the object she'd been working on, popped it into her bag and stood.

He didn't make eye contact as she walked to the elevators and stood to one side. She nodded at them when the doors opened and they entered first. She stepped in and leaned against the side closest to the controls.

"I'm starving." Caroline rummaged through her purse. "I was in the middle of dinner with Stephanie when Mom called."

"Stephanie?"

Caroline flushed.

"You said you had a date."

"I did…sort of."

"With Stephanie?" Caroline and Stephanie had been inseparable friends since preschool.

"She's due any day. We wanted to get in one girls' night before the baby."

Blake shook his head. "I get that. What I don't get is why you told me you had a date."

Caroline pulled a half-eaten granola bar from her bag. "Yes! Now I won't pass out before I get back to Stephanie's."

"You're spending the night?"

Caroline shrugged. "You know, in case she goes into labor or something."

"You still haven't answered my question."

Caroline took a huge bite and chewed. She pointed to her mouth, as if she planned to answer his question after she swallowed. He didn't buy it.

"You aren't getting out of this, Care Bear," he said. "I don't care if you date or not. I do care about you lying to me."

He glanced at Heidi. She was watching Caroline, her eyes narrowed in clear concern. Maybe he should save the brotherly lecture for later. Someplace private. Someplace where he could give his little sister a real piece of his mind. He rested his head against the wall and stared at the ceiling. Had he put so much pressure on her that she'd rather lie to him than admit she hadn't had a date in a year? Maybe he owed her an apology.

"Blake!" Heidi's voice cut through his thoughts. Why was she yelling at him? Caroline would—

"It's okay. We'll get you some help." Heidi had her arms around Caroline, supporting her. His sister looked like she was barely holding on to consciousness. "I've got you," Heidi said. "Peanut allergy, right?"

How did she know? He put his arm around Caroline and together they eased her into a sitting position on the elevator floor. "Yes. Peanuts. Caroline? Care Bear, can you hear me?"

Caroline's eyes were open, but she didn't seem to be able to speak. Her face was red and her lips had a slight purplish cast.

"Does she carry an EpiPen?" Heidi rummaged through Caroline's purse.

"She should. She always has it."

Heidi flipped the purse over and shook everything out.

"It's not here!" She shoved the contents back into the purse, then jumped to her feet and pressed the emergency button as the doors opened into the lobby of the hospital.

"How do we get to the emergency room?" Heidi shouted at the startled volunteer sitting at the reception desk.

The woman pointed to her right. Blake spotted a wheelchair and didn't bother asking if he could take it. As soon as Caroline was seated he took off down the hall.

"Call somebody and tell them we're coming," Heidi ordered the receptionist as they raced past her. "Tell them it's anaphylaxis and we'll need some epinephrine."

The next few minutes passed in a blur of yelling and questions he had no answers to. What had she eaten? How had she been exposed?

The ER staff was amazing and it wasn't long before Caroline sat up on a bed taking deep breaths through the oxygen mask she pressed to her face. Tears streaked her ashen cheeks.

"My EpiPen?" she asked, her voice rough.

"It wasn't in your purse," he said.

"I know it was," she said, confusion and fear thickening her words.

"Heidi dumped everything out, Caroline. It wasn't there."

Caroline glanced around the room. "Who's Heidi?"

Uh-oh. What should he say? Once they'd stabilized Caroline, Heidi had slipped from the room. He couldn't tell Caroline he suspected she'd gone to do some sort of special agent undercover something or other.

"The lady in the elevator."

"Oh," Caroline said. "Do you know her?"

Did he? Not really. "We just met." He needed to change the subject. "Why don't you rest. Don't try to talk. Focus on breathing."

Her eyes fluttered closed. "That's not going to be too difficult."

Within minutes, her soft snores blended with the beeping from the monitors. She'd never had much tolerance for Benadryl, and he had a feeling they'd pumped her full of it. His phone buzzed in his pocket and he was surprised to see the initials *HZ* pop up.

He stepped from the room and caught the call. "Hello?"

"How's Caroline?" Heidi's words came out clipped.

"Stable. They want to watch her, but she should be able to go home in a few hours."

"Okay. Good." The relief in her words surprised him. During the entire chaotic episode she'd been calm and composed. Even as she yelled for assistance, the words came out with authority, not panic.

Had she been more worried than he'd realized?

"I need to talk to her."

"What? Why?"

"Because," she said, and her voice dropped to a whisper. "Three members of your family have experienced life-threatening catastrophes in the past thirty-six hours. Do you not think that's a problem?"

"Of course it's a problem, but shouldn't we call the police?"

"My boss already has. They've turned it over to us."

That was fast. "Who is 'us'?"

"The FBI in general, my team in specific. My partner is on his way from DC, along with several other agents who are coming to provide round-the-clock protection for your family."

This could not be happening. It had to be a dream. He would wake up and his biggest problem would be a malfunctioning blower at the factory.

"Do you think she's up to talking to me?"

"She's asleep, and with the amount of Benadryl they gave her, I doubt that status will change anytime soon." He pressed his head against the wall as another thought raced through his mind. "Oh, man. I need to tell Mom and Dad. And I need to call Caroline's friend Stephanie to let her know what's going on."

Then another, far greater fear threatened to choke him. "Maggie."

"I'm sorry? What?"

"Maggie. I need to get her. She's not safe. She's—"

"Blake." A hand closed over his arm and it took him a second to realize that her voice hadn't come through the phone. How had she snuck up on him?

Heidi squeezed Blake's arm. Poor guy. He was handling this far better than she'd anticipated, but he looked like he was about to drop.

"Maggie is fine." She released his arm. "Two of the best agents I know are currently posing as repairmen. They are watching the front and back of your in-laws' home. The windows and blinds are open enough for them to see Maggie and your in-laws. No one will get in there without going through my agents."

No need to tell him that if anything happened to a child, none of them would ever forgive themselves.

"Why is this happening?"

She didn't think he'd meant to say that aloud, but it was a valid question. "I don't know, but I will find out. It would help me if you could tell me everything you know about Caroline's allergy. It looked like she reacted to something in her purse. Could she have purchased something with peanuts in it by accident?"

"No. Caroline is supercautious. She special-orders those bars by the case. They are crazy expensive, made in a guaranteed nut-free production facility. She has one every day. She eats half in the morning and the other half in the afternoon."

"No allergies other than peanuts, right?"

"No. She eats dairy, eggs, shellfish…no problem. She can even eat almonds or cashews. Wait a minute. How do you know that?"

Oops. "It's in her file."

Blake rubbed his eyes. "Awesome."

He needed sleep, but she couldn't do anything about that. A small arrangement of chairs sat in a quiet corner and she nodded in their direction. "Let's sit."

He didn't argue. He collapsed into a chair and put his elbows on his knees and his face in his hands. "I can't believe she didn't have her EpiPen."

"Is she good about keeping it with her?"

"Fanatical. She had a severe reaction when she was twelve. The pen was at the house and we were up at the waterfall behind the plant. Big company-wide fun day. She bit into a dessert and her throat closed up. We've always been thankful for the presence and quick thinking of one of our operators with a serious bee allergy. He had his pen in his pocket. I've never seen anyone move the way he did. Saved her life."

He blew out a breath and looked at her, frustration and confusion evident on his face. "Since then, she doesn't go anywhere without it. She keeps one in her purse at all times, we have two in the plant medical supplies, and she carries one around in her pocket when she's at home. You saw how fast it happened. If she had a serious reaction when she was alone…"

Heidi could imagine. And the more Blake talked, the more certain she'd become that this had not been an accident.

"Do people at the plant know about the allergy?"

"Yeah. We don't prohibit people from eating peanuts, but we do have a peanut-free break room and general allergy awareness as part of our new employee orientation.

We have two people with peanut allergies, one with a bee allergy and another with an egg allergy."

He fiddled with his watch band. "Do you think it was Mark?"

Oh, yeah. But she couldn't prove it. "He's at the top of my suspect list. Her allergy is well-known. Is it safe to assume her 'half a bar at a time' habit is common knowledge, as well?"

"The guys tease her about it. Tell her it wouldn't hurt her to finish the whole bar in one sitting."

"Who are these guys? Are you talking about people who work for you?"

"You have to understand. There are two guys who have worked for HPI since before we were born and about fifteen of our employees have been with us since I was in elementary school. They've watched us grow up and they don't have a problem telling Caroline she needs to eat more, or get a boyfriend, or take a vacation."

"Do they treat you the same way?"

He laughed. "They tell me I need to lay off the Mountain Dew. And get remarried."

Remarried? Interesting.

"Neither of those things are going to happen."

Even more interesting. Pro–Mountain Dew, antimarriage? Or just antimarriage for himself?

"You take your Mountain Dew that seriously?"

"Yep."

He didn't elaborate, and Heidi pulled the conversation back to Caroline. "I'm going to have the wrapper and the remainder of the bar analyzed, but the circumstantial evidence indicates someone contaminated it with peanuts. If we go with that theory, would it be safe to assume they would have expected her to finish it yesterday while she was still at the plant?"

"I guess—" His brow furrowed.

"What?"

"She always finishes it. Every day. And she seemed surprised to find a half in her purse."

Heidi didn't like where this was going. "Do people know what brand or what flavor she likes? And would it be possible for someone to get access to her purse?"

Blake groaned. "Two weeks ago."

"What happened two weeks ago?"

"One of the guys has a granddaughter with a peanut allergy and he asked Caroline about her granola bars during a shift-change meeting. I only remember it because she borrowed my phone and pulled up the website she orders from to show him. They were talking about the brand, which flavors she likes, stuff like that."

His Adam's apple bobbed. "Mark was there."

Heidi closed her eyes and tried to pull the events of the past thirty-six hours together. "Pure speculation here, but let's run with it. Markos buys one of Caroline's favorite flavors, opens the package, breaks off half and then, what? Puts peanuts in it? Wouldn't she have noticed?"

Heidi pictured the scene in the elevator. The conversation, Caroline looking through her purse, finding the granola bar. Heidi continued to reason, "No, not tonight. She didn't even look. She pulled the wrapper back an inch and took a bite. But he couldn't have known she wouldn't look at it. If he wanted to be sure she wouldn't notice, he would have used something fine—peanut dust, tiny flecks of peanut, maybe he even used peanut oil, and dipped the granola bar in it and then slid it back in the wrapper. Would she react to an amount that small?"

Blake nodded. "It would be enough. She's so sensitive to peanuts that we can't eat in a restaurant with peanuts on the table or shells on the floor. The oils in the air will make her face tingle."

"So he contaminates a bar and puts it in her purse? How did it get in her purse? Does she leave it out at work?"

He grimaced and nodded again. "We've never had a problem with theft. She leaves her purse in her office most of the time. Sometimes she brings it with her to the shift-change meeting if she's leaving for an appointment or something."

"What kind of appointments?"

"Any kind."

"Personal or professional?"

"Either. Caroline is our Chief Financial Officer. The way our organization is structured, the sales and accounting staff all report to her. So she could be meeting with anyone from the people who service our printers to the clients who buy our finished product. Or she could have a dentist appointment. She doesn't have a standing appointment on any one day, if that's what you're asking. Every day is different."

"So maybe she brought her purse to a shift-change meeting and he slipped the contaminated bar in there?"

Would Caroline have noticed? Heidi didn't know. She had to remind herself that the average American didn't walk around assuming people were trying to kill them. An extra half of a granola bar wouldn't look like a weapon. It would look like a snack.

"Did she leave early any day this week?"

Blake leaned back and rubbed his neck. "Maybe? I can't remember."

Heidi didn't push him. Sometimes memories eluded people when they were stressed or fatigued, and Blake Harrison was both.

"Thursday," Blake said after a few moments.

"What happened Thursday?"

"She had a hair appointment. I remember because I was

annoyed that she was leaving." He shook his head and Heidi could see the remorse on his face.

"Hey, don't beat yourself up."

"I need to tell her I'm sorry."

Heidi didn't know what to make of this guy. Smart. Strong. Stubborn. And a sensitive family guy? She'd always thought guys like this were an urban legend. Or a fairy tale.

Not that it mattered. She didn't have time for fairy tales.

"You can apologize later. I think for now, we need to focus on why on earth someone is trying to take out your family. Because there's a strong possibility that whoever put the granola bar in her purse also took her EpiPen. If that's true, then we've got a bigger problem than we thought."

"Which is?"

"They weren't trying to scare her or distract her. They were trying to kill her."

FIVE

As Sunday morning dawned, Blake drove Caroline home in her car. "What about your car?"

"We'll get it later," he said.

Caroline didn't respond. If she hadn't been loopy from the medication, she would have pressed him about the car.

Heidi's Acura flitted in and out of his rearview mirror until he pulled into his driveway. He caught a glimpse as she drove past.

She'd promised to return in thirty minutes with food. And then they would talk.

She'd been there all night at the hospital. Again. Some of the time she'd spent in the waiting room, knitting what he now knew to be a scarf. Other times she'd disappear and he assumed she was talking to her team about the chaos that had descended into their world.

Before Caroline had been released, she'd introduced him to two men in scrubs.

FBI agents in scrubs.

They'd assured him they would stay with his mom and dad and would contact Heidi with anything suspicious.

Father, please protect them. Protect all of us.

Where had that prayer come from? He and God hadn't been on great terms for a while. He'd never stopped believing. He knew God was in control, but with everything that had happened with Lana, it felt as though God had let him down.

Still, in this moment, he knew there was no higher power he could turn to. He couldn't protect everyone he loved, no matter how much he wanted to or how hard he tried. Even Heidi, with her ever-growing team of FBI agents, couldn't guarantee their safety.

Father, please.

There wasn't anything else he could say.

"You okay?" Caroline asked as he parked in his driveway and scanned the lawn and surrounding woods.

"Tired."

"I wish you would take me to my house."

"Mom wants you to stay with me." While true, it wasn't the real reason he'd insisted on having Caroline spend the rest of the day with him.

"I'm not four years old."

Caroline could pout like a champ, but her drama had no effect on him. Not today. Besides, when Heidi returned and said what she needed to say, Caroline's objections would disintegrate.

Twenty minutes later, a sharp rap on his door pulled his attention away from the pantry. A pantry full of food that might kill him if it had been contaminated. How hard would it have been for Mark to break into his house and slip poison into his food? Maybe not the canned goods, but the bread? The open cereal boxes and cookies taunted him. He would throw that stuff away. Too risky.

"Were you expecting someone?" Caroline shifted on the couch. He nodded, but didn't offer any other reply.

He checked the peephole and opened the door for Heidi.

She stood at the door, two huge boxes in her hands. "I understand the Schwinns' bakery is a peanut-free facility," she said as she stepped inside.

She placed the boxes on the coffee table and stuck her hand out in Caroline's direction. "Hi. I'm Heidi Zimmerman."

Caroline's confused gaze bounced from the boxes to Heidi to Blake and made the circuit again before she took Heidi's hand. "Caroline Harrison. Nice to meet you." Uncertainty laced her words.

Heidi tilted her head in his direction. "You didn't tell her?"

Blake cleared his throat. He'd intended to, but—

Heidi reached into her pocket and held her badge out for Caroline's inspection. "Then please accept my apologies, Ms. Harrison. I thought your brother would have given you a heads-up." He heard annoyance and understanding in her words. "Let's start again. Special Agent Heidi Zimmerman. I'm with the FBI, and I'm sorry to have to tell you this, but I'm concerned that someone is trying to kill your family."

Caroline glared at Blake. "I knew something... How could you fail to mention... How long have you known—"

"Could I make a suggestion?" Heidi opened the boxes on the table, revealing doughnuts, bagels and even a stack of chocolate chip cookies. "In my experience, it's best not to dive into a deep conversation without fortifying yourself first. Doughnut?"

She looked through the box. "Chocolate glazed? Lemon filled?"

Caroline continued to glare at Blake, but she accepted a chocolate éclair and he grabbed a cinnamon twist. As soon as they had food in their mouths, Heidi brought Caroline up to speed.

He'd thought hearing it for the second time wouldn't be too bad, but watching Caroline absorb the news made it all much worse.

Thirty minutes and multiple doughnuts later, Caroline looked at him and whispered, "What on earth are we going to do? We can't dump this on mom and dad. Not now."

Heidi took a bite of a chocolate chip cookie and he got the impression she was giving herself time to think.

He'd been thinking a lot, too. This might be his best chance to throw out his plan. "I've got an idea," he said. Both women looked at him. Caroline looked surprised, Heidi wary.

He pointed at Heidi. "You said you have an engineering degree?"

"Yes. Why?"

"What if you come work for us?"

"Work for you?"

"Yes. We could hire you as a consultant or something. You'd have an excuse to be around all the time. You could get to know Mark. Learn the process. Maybe figure out why he wanted to work for us." He looked at Caroline. "We won't say anything to Mom and Dad until Dad's home. Or until we don't have any other choice. Whichever comes first. I hate keeping anything from them, especially something this big, but I know they'll understand once we explain."

Caroline nodded her agreement.

Heidi took another bite. "It's not a bad idea," she said after she swallowed. "Not bad at all."

Caroline smirked in his direction. He knew that look. She was up to something. Something he wouldn't like. She smiled at Heidi. "You should stay here on the property."

What? Oh, no. He knew where this was going.

Heidi shook her head. "I don't think that's a good—"

"Hear me out. We have a small little A-frame that we used to use as a guesthouse. We've always called it the cabin and I think it would be perfect for you. It has a kitchen and a living room downstairs and the bedroom and bathroom are upstairs in the loft. It needs a little bit of work to make it habitable, but I could have it ready in two days. Then you'd be right by the plant, and by us. You'd be able to provide some security for us while figuring out what Mark's up to." She bit into a doughnut hole, a triumphant gleam in her eyes as she smiled at Blake. This was payback for all the times he'd nagged her about going out more, opening herself up to the idea of meeting someone.

Heidi took another bite of her cookie, but her eyes never left his face. She must be waiting to see what he thought of Caroline's plan. The short answer—not much. He knew his sister and she never failed to seize an opportunity to try to entangle him with a woman.

The worst part of it was that he didn't see how he could get out of it this time.

"Where are you staying?" If she were nearby—

She gave the name of her hotel. "Takes me about twenty minutes to get here."

Twenty minutes. If anything terrible happened, she couldn't get here in time to stop it. Although she did seem to have a gift for being in the right place at the right time.

But…he didn't know her. Didn't know for sure if he could trust her. Although the whole lifesaving bit made it hard not to.

He tried to read her face, but she did a great job of keeping her thoughts hidden. "I guess it's up to you," he said. "If you want to stay here, you're more than welcome to the cabin. Although you might not want it after you see it."

An hour later, Heidi slid her phone back into her pocket and smiled at Blake. "We've got a green light for your plan to hire me as a consultant. We need to fine-tune things a bit, but if you believe you can sell it to your staff, then it's worth a shot."

Blake nodded from the recliner he'd been dozing in. "That's great. Do we need to talk now?"

Caroline rolled over on the couch. "I can wake up. I think," she said, sleep thick in her voice.

"No." Heidi looked at her watch. It was 9:30 a.m. When

had she slept last? Her poor body wouldn't know what to
do if it ever got a decent night's rest. "We all need to sleep."
She stifled a yawn. "Why don't we plan to meet tonight.
Around eight?"

"Eight's fine."

"Okay. Then I'm going to head out." Heidi stood and
retrieved her jacket from the back of the couch.

The slam of the recliner being pushed back into a sitting
position startled her and her hand flew to her back. Maybe
Blake wouldn't notice?

"Are you armed?"

So much for that "not noticing" idea. "Yes. I'm always
armed."

Her statement might have been more troublesome a few
hours ago, but instead of concern, relief flashed across
Blake's face. Given everything he'd been through, he had
to appreciate having someone prepared to defend them.
Which reminded her—

"Do you have a gun in the house?"

"Two. A 9 mm and a shotgun."

"Loaded?" She appreciated the need for safety, but under
the circumstances, an unloaded weapon wouldn't do them
much good.

"Yes. Out of reach of Maggie, but yes."

Good.

Blake hefted himself out of the recliner and winced.
Still sore from Friday's adventure, no doubt. "Are you sure
you're okay to drive? I could give you a lift."

Wow. Contrary to what she'd believed, chivalry was not
dead. At least not where Blake Harrison was concerned.

It was a fair question. Keeping her eyes open was requir-
ing a massive amount of willpower and she'd crossed into
the zone where she could be a danger to herself and others if she didn't sleep soon. On the other hand, she didn't

think Blake was in much better shape, and he hadn't had the training to teach him to power through the fatigue.

"I think I'll make it." She could hear her uncertainty.

Blake pursed his lips. "I don't like it. You're welcome to crash here. Get a few hours and then go to your hotel."

Tempting. But he was in the recliner. Caroline snored on the couch. The only other options were the beds and there was no way she was sleeping in their beds. Besides, she needed a shower and a change of clothes, both of which required a trip to her hotel.

"I appreciate it, but I'll be okay. I'll call my team and get a few things rolling. That will keep me awake."

Blake clearly wasn't pleased, but he didn't argue.

She dialed her team before she pulled out of the driveway and it took the entire twenty minutes to her hotel and an additional fifteen after she'd secured herself in her room to get things lined up to her satisfaction. She grabbed a shower and fell across the hotel bed.

Over the next twelve hours, a team of agents would descend on Etowah, North Carolina. They'd come in trucks and minivans and SUVs and they'd be dressed as repairmen and nurses and accountants.

They would have two jobs. Protect the Harrisons.

And bring down the Kovacs.

Heidi pulled into the Harrison driveway at 7:50 p.m. She'd gotten six hours of sleep. Not as much as she needed, but not so much that she wouldn't be able to sleep tonight.

A rush of adrenaline coursed through her as she took the three steps to Blake's front porch. She attributed it to her excitement about the way this assignment was taking shape. She ignored the way her stomach flipped when Blake opened the door.

"Everything okay?" She scanned the room.

"Great," he said and flashed her a smile. Her stomach flipped again. What was with her? "Come on in."

His phone rang and he glanced at it. "It's Caroline. She's at the hospital with Mom," he said.

"Please, take it."

As Blake stepped onto the porch to take the call, a small blond head peaked out from the hallway. Heidi glimpsed a pink-clad foot, then an elbow. Then a pair of twinkling eyes met Heidi's. No doubt about it. Maggie Harrison.

"Hello." At Heidi's greeting, the little girl sprang into the room.

"Hello! You're Heidi, aren't you? I'm glad you're here. You have a lot of hair. I'm Maggie. I want a dog, but Daddy says not yet. Do you have a dog?"

Heidi knelt down to eye level with Maggie. "I do have a lot of hair. My godfather says I have one curl for every time I've made him smile." She paused and put on her most grieved expression. "I'm afraid I do not have a dog. Do you think we could be friends anyway?"

The little girl launched herself at Heidi and threw her arms around her neck. Unprepared for the miniature assault, Heidi wrapped one arm around Maggie and allowed them to roll back onto the floor.

Maggie jumped up giggling. "I knocked you over! I'm sorry! Are you hurt?" She proceeded to pace around Heidi in a wide circle, examining her for injuries. "Did you bump your head?" A tiny hand reached out toward Heidi's hair, but paused.

Maggie was clearly intrigued by her curls, but not quite brave enough to touch them without permission. Heidi stifled a laugh. "I'm not sure. Maybe you should check for bumps."

Maggie wasted no time and began a full inspection, lifting curls and patting them back into place. "I think you'll be okay," she said with authority.

"Whew! That's a relief. Help me up, will you?" Maggie took her hands and pulled with gusto.

Heidi had almost regained her footing when Blake stepped back inside.

"Daddy!" Maggie ran straight for her father and jumped into his arms. He spun her around several times before squeezing her tight and setting her on her feet. "I knocked Heidi over!"

"You did what?"

"I knocked her over!" She hooted with laughter. "She doesn't have a dog, but we can still be friends."

"I'm glad you're going to be friends, but you shouldn't call an adult by their first name, Maggie-moo. Can you say Ms. Zimmerman?"

"Ms. Zimzezan—"

"Zim-mer-man." Blake sounded out each syllable.

"Zimzemaz."

Heidi bit her lips together and Blake seemed amused. Could she intervene without interfering? When Blake glanced her way, she mouthed, "Heidi is fine."

Blake shook his head in defeat. "Maybe we could go with Miss Heidi."

Maggie's smile lit the room. "Much easier." She turned to Heidi. "You've got a big name."

Blake looked like he wanted to crawl through a hole in the floor.

Heidi found Maggie's exuberance refreshing. She directed her words to Maggie. "It is a big name. Some of my close friends call me 'Z' for short."

"I like 'Z'!"

Blake shook his head. "I think 'Miss Heidi' will do fine. Why don't you go brush your teeth."

"Yes, sir." Maggie raced away. "Daddy?" she yelled from down the hall.

"Yes, pumpkin."

"I think you're wrong about her hair. I don't think her hair got curly because she put her finger in a socket. I think she was born with it."

Oh…he would pay for that.

"Sorry," Blake said.

Heidi gave up trying not to laugh. "She's really something," she said.

"You have no idea." He pointed down the hall. "She was supposed to be in bed thirty minutes ago. When she heard you were coming over, she came up with every excuse imaginable to stall."

"What did you tell her about me? Besides that I'd stuck my finger in a socket."

He had the grace to flush. "I told her Aunt Caroline and I had made a new friend. That you were going to be working at the plant and you'd be staying in the cabin as soon as Caroline gets it fixed up."

Sounded like a story a five-year-old could accept. "We'll need to improve on that if we're going to convince your employees," she said.

They spent the next two hours working on their cover story. When Heidi left, the plan was as fully formed as an off-the-cuff mission could be expected to be. She'd have to be herself as much as possible. There wasn't time to develop a detailed legend.

She'd use her own engineering credentials and her own name. She was coming into HPI as a quality consultant. Blake didn't think it would be too difficult for the staff to believe he'd hired someone, given the issues they'd had over the past few weeks.

The timing was the trickiest part. She needed to start this week, but if she showed up saying she'd agreed to take the job without even touring the plant and submitting a proposal first, it might jeopardize her credibility.

They landed on a solution neither of them liked. They

wouldn't bring it up, but if anyone asked, they'd say she and Blake had been talking about her coming for a while, and she'd had a cancellation in her schedule that allowed her to work them in before the holidays. It was weak, but if she was only around for a little while, maybe it would hold.

SIX

Heidi slept a dreamless seven hours. When she woke on Monday morning, her first order of business was to be sure everyone had survived the night. Jeffrey Harrison continued to recover and should come home in the next few days. They'd managed to avoid burdening the senior Harrisons with the Kovac drama thus far, but that would all change soon. Blake and Caroline had agreed that once their dad was home, both parents must be told. Heidi found the family dynamics fascinating.

The family was certainly wealthy. Privileged, compared to most. Yet no one could accuse either of the Harrison children of being weak, spoiled or suffering from a heavy case of entitlement.

Blake had told her that while Jeffrey still had the ultimate say in what happened at HPI, he was methodically training both Blake and Caroline in all aspects of the business.

So while Blake was in charge of engineering and Caroline handled sales and finance, either of them could step in and manage the facilities or human resources if they needed to. They knew their business inside and out, worked well together and, in their early thirties, were more than capable of running the entire operation on their own.

But Heidi was used to being around people who were

good at their jobs. The FBI recruited the best of the best, and she would—and had—put her life in the hands of her team without hesitation. What she had trouble comprehending was the warmth of the family relationship. Caroline and Blake worked hard and were committed to their jobs, the factory and their employees, but their dedication to HPI couldn't match their devotion to their loved ones. The siblings were so close, so invested in each other's happiness and well-being and so protective of each other that it was almost hard to believe they were for real.

And their respect for both parents touched her in ways she couldn't understand. It had become clear during the evening that both of them longed to have their parents' advice and insights into the situation with the Kovacs.

She couldn't help but wonder if she and Rach would have been like this. Calling up the Thompsons for advice on major life decisions, confident their advice would be full of wisdom and love.

Heidi stuffed all thoughts of the Thompsons deep, along with all the emotion that came with them.

She'd come to North Carolina for justice. To see the Kovacs answer for their crimes—against the Thompsons and the untold others who'd had the misfortune of crossing their path. She hadn't expected to be faced with the challenge of protecting another innocent family from them.

She could not fail.

She spent the day poring over the case files she'd brought with her from DC, as well as researching the production of plastic containers online. She'd even checked out entries on Wikipedia and videos on YouTube.

She spoke to Blake twice. Once to assure him that the agents guarding Maggie at school had reported no difficulties and had even managed to get eyes on her by hacking into a webcam. That part wouldn't make it into any reports.

She didn't know who'd pulled off the hack. She doubted they had permission.

Right now, she didn't care.

Her second phone call confirmed that everything was in place for her to arrive the next day.

As she pulled into the parking lot of HPI on Tuesday morning, she ran through the script in her head, reminding herself of the role she was playing. And why.

She parked and checked all the gadgets and devices that came with running an undercover operation.

Nine o'clock. Showtime.

Blake had suggested she start her first day after the regular 8:00 a.m. meeting so he could explain her presence to his engineering team, and also take the focus off her arrival. She stepped out of her car, paused to pull her sleeves down until they covered her elbows and confirmed her pants hadn't snagged in the ankle holster. That would be a great way to start the day.

"You look good, kiddo," she heard through the earpiece connecting her to her team. Ah. Uncle Frank. Of course he would be checking in on her transmissions this morning. He'd been itching to get eyes on Markos Kovac. And today, she planned to get up close and personal.

She had cameras hidden in her shirt buttons and earrings. Her watch and necklace had microphones that Max could turn on and off as needed. "Cameras are operational, Z." Max was monitoring everything from a cable company van parked down the road. "Give me a cough so I can check your mic."

Heidi cleared her throat instead.

"Got to be in charge, don't ya."

She would have made a snide remark, but someone might be watching and she didn't want to be seen talking to herself this early in the game.

"Fine. Do it your way. We've got your back."

Heidi scanned the parking lot and buildings. *Father, open my eyes. Show me what he's up to. Help me see what isn't there. Hear the words no one has spoken. Know the plan before it's implemented. Help me, Abba.*

She stepped into the office area and was greeted with a strained but polite "Good morning. Are you Ms. Zimmerman?"

"I am, yes. Please, call me Heidi."

"I'm Bridget. I'm the office manager. Come on in and I'll—"

Bridget's phone buzzed. "Yes, Blake?…Of course." Heidi got the impression that Bridget would do anything Blake asked.

The sweetness in Bridget's tone and the dreamy look in her eyes disappeared as she addressed Heidi. "Ms. Zimmerman, Mr. Harrison is tied up on the production floor at the moment. He says he'll be with you as soon as he can. Feel free to have a seat."

"Thank you, Bridget." She tried to infuse the words with sincerity and kindness.

Heidi took one of the offered chairs and mentally reviewed what she knew about Bridget. Twenty-four. Degree in business administration from UNC Asheville. Did an internship at HPI during her senior year and came to work right after graduation to replace the retiring office manager.

The file hadn't made mention of her having a crush on her boss, but that was exactly why human intelligence was necessary.

Did Bridget have any idea how transparent her feelings were? Heidi hated to put the poor girl through unnecessary stress, but how could she explain she posed no threat to anyone's future happiness? The last thing she needed was a relationship to complicate her already complex existence.

Ten minutes later, Bridget's phone buzzed again.

"Yes, Blake?…Of course."

"You can go in now, Ms. Zimmerman." Bridget indicated the door with Blake's name stenciled on it.

Heidi tapped on the door.

"Come in," Blake said. "Close the door, if you don't mind, Ms. Zimmerman."

They'd discussed this last night. In the office, there could be no familiarity. Not yet. According to their cover story, they knew each other only by phone calls and reputation. Still, she hadn't expected not to like the professional version of Blake.

She closed the door and took in her surroundings. The back wall of the office was solid glass with a phenomenal view of fall foliage. The walls to either side were dotted with diplomas and photographs of waterfalls.

"How did you get in here without me seeing you?"

Blake grinned and pointed to a door on Heidi's right. "Dad's office is through that door." He pointed to a door on her left. "Your office is through that door. From your office I can get into Caroline's office, and from her office, I can get into a back hall that leads to a staircase that goes straight to the plant floor."

He pointed toward the door that led into the reception area. "I don't normally walk through everyone else's office on my way to mine, but I didn't want to have to pretend I'd never met you in front of Bridget."

"Probably a good idea."

Blake laughed.

"Is everything okay?" Heidi asked. "Bridget said you were tied up on the production floor."

Blake blew out a breath. "Yes. No. We have a new piece of equipment. A blower. It's a critical component in the production of those ball-shaped water bottles I told you about. But that thing has been giving me fits for the past couple of weeks."

Blake handed her a folder from his desk before returning to his seat. "Anyway, I've taken the liberty of planning your first day. I hope that's okay." He tapped a button on his phone. "Bridget?"

"Yes, Blake?"

"Could you call Eric to the office?"

"Of course."

He picked up a stapled stack of papers from his desk. "Eric is our lead engineer. He knows the process inside and out. As we discussed, the best way for you to understand our quality issues is to understand our process. Eric will show you our Receiving area where you'll see how we process our raw materials. Then he'll walk you through the production facility and then out to Shipping. That should take you through the morning."

He flipped to the next page. "After lunch, Caroline will give you an overview of our sales structure. And at 3:00 p.m. I'll take you down for our shift-change meeting. That's the only time all of our shift supervisors are here at the same time and you can meet everyone."

That's when she'd come face-to-face with Markos Kovac. Organized-crime brat by day. Second-shift production supervisor by night.

Blake's phone buzzed. "Blake, Eric is here."

"Send him in."

Eric opened the door to the office. Fifties, bald, pudgy, intense eyes. The eyes gave him away as someone with specialized training. She'd been told she had those eyes herself. She knew all about Eric from his file. Married, two kids, first grandchild on the way. Former military, special forces. Blake had chosen well when he'd teamed them up. Who knew what Eric had noticed?

Let the games begin.

At 2:45 p.m. Heidi adjusted the height of the chair behind her desk. Not that she'd spent any time behind it today. This morning she'd watched as tiny plastic chips, some solid white, others translucent with a slight bluish tinge, flowed from a tanker truck into large hoppers positioned at the beginning of each production line.

Eric had shown her the bays where they received raw materials and the storage facilities for each product. The inventory system impressed her. Bar codes and GPS tracking devices allowed Eric to pinpoint the location of any item in the warehouse.

It was all remarkable, but nothing she'd seen explained why an organized-crime family would take enough of an interest that they would place their youngest grandson in the production facility. She rubbed her temples. If it were easy, they'd have nailed them fifteen years ago.

"You okay, Z?" Max had been silent most of the day. He knew how hard it could be to carry on conversations with someone chattering in your ear.

She clicked her tongue twice, their prearranged signal for yes.

"Liar."

The tap on her door forced her to swallow her retort. She waved Blake in.

"You ready?"

So many layers in those two words.

Caroline had left for the hospital right after their meeting, which meant Blake was the only person, if she didn't count the fifty listening and watching, who had any idea what was happening here. Or how critical the next few minutes would be.

"Absolutely."

They walked to the production floor and into the small office area at the back of the building. Blake held the door. "Ladies first."

A gentleman? Or did he assume she'd want to be the first in? Either way, she gave him the briefest nod as she walked into the room.

"Easy." Max again.

One deep breath, one cheery smile, one "I'm a quality consultant and I'm only here to make your lives better" persona, coming right up. She moved through the room, shaking hands, making introductions until she got to him. "Heidi Zimmerman."

"Mark Hammond. Nice to meet you. Welcome." She'd seen his picture, been watching him for over a month, but she'd never heard his voice before. She'd had no idea he sounded so much like his older brother. The voice of a long-lost friend coming from the mouth of an enemy sent a swell of anger coursing through her system. She hadn't anticipated such a visceral reaction and she had to pause a few moments to quell it.

"Thank you."

In the press of people, it was easy to bump into Markos a couple of times as she maneuvered around a chair. The second bump was perfect.

One tiny transmitter on one not-so-tiny criminal. Then it was on to the next person around the table.

"That was anticlimactic," Max said.

When all the introductions were made and everyone found a seat, Heidi wound up across from Blake and three seats away from Markos.

The transmitter would work as long as it stayed on Markos's jacket. It could still be functioning in July unless he ran it through the wash or got caught in the rain.

A few months. Heidi tried to keep her focus on the conversation around the room, but she couldn't help but wonder how long she'd be here. Days? Maybe a few weeks. Months? Not likely.

Not likely at all.

By Friday, they'd fallen into a routine. One he couldn't have envisioned when he'd walked out of the plant one week ago.

Had it really only been a week?

He already struggled to remember what life had been like before Heidi had burst into his world.

Heidi attended the morning meeting with him. Then she spent the day out on the plant floor. Shadowing, she called it. She'd shadowed three operators, two engineers and one shift supervisor. The line operators all had a crush on her.

Then she'd attend the afternoon meeting with him before returning to her office for an hour. Doing what, he didn't know. Then she'd tap on his door, say good-night and head to the cabin.

Caroline had taken a dingy, dated space and made the most of the time she'd had to bring the cabin into the twenty-first century. A fresh coat of paint—he did not want to know how much she'd paid the painters to get it done that fast—and some new furnishings from IKEA and her favorite consignment store, and it was ready for Heidi.

She'd moved in on Wednesday afternoon and if her car's location was an indicator, she spent her evenings in the cabin, but he had his suspicions about how often she stayed inside.

Not that he'd noticed her leaving on foot. Had she dug a tunnel? Or maybe she had access to some new stealth technology and could walk around without being seen?

It didn't matter. Except it did. He couldn't get a read on her. He'd thought they might be moving toward some sort of friendship, but since she'd started working on Tuesday, she'd been all business. No hint she was anyone other than the consultant she was pretending to be. No chitchat.

Except with Maggie. It had taken Maggie all of one afternoon to decide "Miss Heidi is awesome." Before Heidi's arrival, Maggie had frequently begged to go home with the carpool buddy who brought her to the plant each afternoon. But now she hopped out of the car with a smile and a quick "See you tomorrow" before racing inside. She barely acknowledged anyone until she'd seen Heidi. Probably because Heidi always welcomed her in for a chat and a taste of some European chocolate candy bar. Not that she'd offered any of the chocolate to anyone else.

As soon as Maggie settled into the little reading corner he'd set up for her in the office area, Heidi returned to full business mode. He appreciated her work ethic, and he didn't want to give her the third degree, but he did want to know what was going on, if she'd made any progress, how she was settling in. All questions he couldn't seem to find an opportunity to ask during the day.

As they left the Friday meeting, he found himself alone with her in the hallway. "What do you think?" Blake asked.

"I think we have great potential here, Mr. Harrison." She flashed him a smile. "I noticed a glassed-in area above the production line. Is there an observation deck?"

"Yeah. It's been there for years but we never use it anymore. With everything automated, there's not much need."

Her eyes flashed. "No one goes up there?"

"Not that I know of. But the windows are one-way glass, so from the factory floor, you can't tell whether or not anyone's there."

"Could you show me?"

"Now?"

"Do you have somewhere else to be?"

"No. Let's go."

They wound through the back of the warehouse. The door screeched and groaned when he opened it. He batted at a few cobwebs as they climbed. The stairs emptied into a small conference room with three large windows. From this vantage point, he could get an angle on all four production lines from beginning to end.

Heidi walked from one window to the other. After a few passes, she paused. "Where is he?" Heidi leaned close to the glass.

"Who?"

"Markos."

He moved to the far window, scanning the new line. Nothing.

"Do you see him?" Heidi asked from the opposite wall.

"No."

She blew out a breath, frustration evident on her face.

"What's wrong?"

"I'd rather him not know we've been up here. But if I don't know where he is, I can't avoid him. I wouldn't want to risk leaving right as he's walking past the door."

She tapped a few buttons on her phone. Shook her head in disgust.

"What is it now?"

"According to this, Markos is at home."

"No, he isn't—"

"I know. He left his coat at home. The one I have a transmitter on."

"Oh."

"And I'm not live-wired into my team at the moment, either, so I can't ask them to locate him."

Yeah, nothing out of the ordinary about this conversation. Nothing at all.

"I'll have to wait," she announced a minute later.

"I'm sorry?"

"I'm going to wait until he comes back on the floor. Then I'll be able to go out through the warehouse and he won't know I've been up here."

"Right."

"You can go."

"Wouldn't it make more sense for me to stay, too? That way if anyone sees us leaving, I can explain that I was showing this to you."

She shrugged. "Yes, but I'm not going to hold you hostage. You own the place. You can go anywhere you like.

No one would question you if you get caught leaving. They might want to know why I'd been up here."

"Right."

She stood in front of the middle window. "Are you sure they can't see me?"

"Positive."

"Aren't you going to go?"

"I'll wait."

She leaned against the window frame, peering out the one-way glass into the production area. "It could be a while."

"It shouldn't be." Mark shouldn't be away from the plant floor for more than a few minutes. And if he was, then Blake would like to know that himself.

"Suit yourself."

Her eyes narrowed and darted as she observed the activity on the plant floor.

Ten agonizing minutes passed in complete silence. He didn't think he'd ever been in a room with anyone who could go more than a few seconds without speaking, coughing or clearing their throat. Not her. If he believed in extraterrestrials, he might suspect her of being an alien life-form. Not much human in her. He blew out a long breath.

She turned her head and made eye contact through the shadows. "Sorry," she said, turning back to the window. "I'm trying to take advantage of the time by memorizing the process. It's fascinating to watch."

"Yeah," Blake said. "*Fascinating*. The word I use for it every day."

She threw him a cheeky grin. "That's because you're used to it. There's something riveting about the way you can take a pile of something that is, sorry to say, useless, and turn it into something functional and practical. It's beautiful."

"I've never heard anyone wax philosophic about the extrusion process."

She huffed and widened her eyes in false shock. "I don't know why not. Everyone I know does." She laughed. A soft, muted laugh, but a laugh all the same.

She turned away from him again. He preferred that she stay facing him, laughing with him. At least she'd talked to him, broken the silence. "You said you were trying to memorize the process. How?"

"I have a photographic memory."

"Of course you do."

She ignored his snide remark and continued. "I may not understand everything I'm seeing, but if I can watch the process from beginning to end a few times—watch it the way it is supposed to go—then I would notice if something was amiss."

"Okay."

"Enough about me."

Um, no. Not hardly.

"Tell me something about yourself."

"Why would you need me to tell you anything? I'm sure you have a nice thick file. Couldn't you look it up?"

"Your file is a little flat."

He would have been offended, but he caught the twitch of her lips and the way she'd cut her eyes over to him for a split second.

"Are you—are you teasing me?"

"I'm trying. You're making it extraordinarily difficult."

"Sorry."

She laughed again. Soft and low. But she didn't say anything else.

He tried to see her as he had a few moments earlier. The way he'd been thinking of her all week. Cold. Calculating. Clinical. All he could see now was a dimple below the surface of her cheek. She had a quick wit and a ready laugh, given the right circumstances. If he answered her question, would she open up again?

He tried to think of something that wouldn't be in his file. She'd already know his name, birth date, where he went to college. And Lana. She'd know all about Lana. Every gruesome detail of that train wreck. But there had to be more.

"Okay, here's something you don't know about me."

"Lay it on me."

"I love science fiction. Fantasy. That kind of stuff."

"Nice try, but I knew that already."

"They have that in my file?" Who were these people?

"No."

"Then how—"

She looked away from the window and then stared at a point on the wall. Her brow puckered and her eyes fluttered closed. "Boxed sets in your den. Blu-rays. *Lord of the Rings. Firefly. Star Trek*—old and new. *Star Wars.*"

She turned and smiled. "You're reading *The Chronicles of Narnia* to Maggie. And in chronological order, no less. Kudos, by the way."

"Um, thanks."

"And you have a tiny TARDIS on your key ring."

He'd forgotten about the *Doctor Who* key chain Caroline had given him for Christmas.

Heidi smiled. "I don't need a file to tell me you have a geek streak."

A geek? Two could play this game. "It takes one to know one."

She raised her hands in mock surrender and grinned. "Touché."

SEVEN

When she turned back to the window, silence wrapped around them. She could hear him breathing. She tried to ignore it and concentrate on the process. If only she could stop her mind from slipping to the man sitting behind her.

That had been happening a lot, and it needed to stop. It would be easier if she could still see him as a suspect. After all, he had hired a man with a shady background. She'd had to consider the possibility that he was in on whatever it was that the Kovacs had planned. But it hadn't taken long for her to abandon that theory.

Even after the entire Harrison family had been cleared of suspicion, she'd assumed Blake would be like many of the men she'd encountered over the years. Men who had no clue how fortunate they were to come from good homes, stable families. Men who disrespected their mothers, neglected their children and never took responsibility for anything or anyone.

She knew not all men were like that. Her foster dad, the one she claimed, had been the first man to shake her deep-seated opinions about men. Then Uncle Frank. Later, Max.

Yet her tendency to assume the worst in men remained.

But after spending time around Blake, watching him interact with his family, play with Maggie, take care of all his normal duties, plus his dad's responsibilities—oh, and deal with her, the engineer/undercover agent—she couldn't help but be impressed.

She was even—and oh, how she hated to admit this— a little in awe.

Blake Harrison set a high bar. Family man, crazy intelligent, gracious employer, good sense of humor and a face she'd caught herself staring at more than once.

He cleared his throat. "You have a file about me and superior observational skills. I'm not likely to come up with anything you don't already know. Why don't you tell me something about yourself?"

Her breath caught. He never failed to surprise her. She could ignore his request, but she didn't want to be rude. She didn't want to ignore him. She wanted to tell him. She wanted him to know the real her.

"Fall is my favorite time of year." Once she started, the words tumbled out. "The leaves are vibrant, the temps perfect. Still enough daylight to enjoy being outside. I love it. And I love ham sandwiches. With mayo and mustard and American cheese. That's it. Meat and cheese. No tomato. No lettuce. And white bread." She had to swallow hard before continuing. "The way my foster mom made them."

She smiled at him. "How's that?"

"Not bad."

"Not bad?" She filled her voice with indignation. "I thought that was pretty good."

"It was, but…"

"But?"

Blake dropped his head. She got the impression he wrestled with what to say.

"I'm sorry, but I never know how much you say to me is the truth. Part of it? None of it? How much is your cover and how much is you? It's impossible for me to know."

Heidi's stomach twisted at his words. This was why it didn't pay to open up to people. Even when she told the truth, they didn't believe her. Why did she bother? And why on earth did she want this man to know her anyway?

She'd spent all week with her head down and her mind focused on the mission. She didn't have time for interpersonal relationships of any kind and keeping Blake Harrison at a distance would be safer for everyone.

So why did it feel as if a piece of her had shriveled up, crawled into a corner and started crying?

"Heidi, I'm sorry. I was out of line."

She could see the regret on his face. Time to get those walls back up. "No. You're quite right. It's a fair question. Intuitive, in fact. Don't apologize."

He moved toward her, his pace measured.

What on earth?

She refused to move, keeping her expression impassive. He edged closer. What was he trying to do? Pick a fight? He had to know if he invaded her space, he wouldn't walk away unscathed.

And he did know. She could see it in his eyes. He knew she might take him down at any moment, but he kept coming. She held her ground.

He stopped a foot away. "I'll keep apologizing until I remove that look from your face. I feel like a jerk."

"Don't."

"Don't apologize, or don't be a jerk?"

"How about both?"

He stepped between her and the glass, blocking her view of everything but him.

She refused to budge. From where she stood, she could read the brand stamped into the buttons on his shirt. Funny. As a rule, she had no tolerance for physical proximity. She preferred to keep enough space around her to throw a punch or a well-placed kick. Closed-in spaces, throngs of people, made her uncomfortable.

Being this close to Blake made her uncomfortable, but

for different reasons. If she looked up, their faces would be mere inches apart. What if he tried to kiss her?

Kiss her? As if he wanted to kiss her.

"I am sorry."

His soft words rang with sincerity and regret, and something she couldn't quite get a handle on. She needed him to give her some space.

"Apology accepted. Now could you please move? I'm trying to learn something here."

"Fine." He went back to his chair. "I like country music."

She focused on breathing.

"I prefer Krispy Kreme to Dunkin'."

Well, who didn't?

"I'd never left this continent until three years ago. I had planned to go on a tour of Europe after college, but that never happened."

"Why not?" The words popped out without permission and she couldn't get them back. She wouldn't blame him if he didn't answer. They'd strayed into intimate territory.

"Life. Married a crook. Had a baby. Wife went to jail. You know. Life."

She knew enough about life. "Life has a way of messing with you."

"Yep."

This time, the silence was free of tension. It didn't last as long, either.

"I'd never have pegged you for a sci-fi fan. I'd have thought you were into foreign films—"

"Please."

"Opera?"

"No."

"French food?"

Was this what people thought about her? She should let it go. But when she looked at Blake Harrison, she didn't see anything more than genuine curiosity. No agenda other than friendship. Friendships were a rare commodity in her world.

She walked to another window and watched the process from a new angle. Might as well tell him the truth. "I lived with a family when I was eight. The mom was from Honduras. She made the most amazing food. It's still my favorite." That family had been great. She might have stayed with them, had it not been for the breast cancer that took the mom too young.

She paused for a few seconds. "I like all kinds of music, but when I want to relax, I listen to Sinatra."

She leaned against the glass. "I love movies, but I hate going to theaters. Dangerous places." Great. Scare the man off from movies forever. "I mean, they aren't, but I get claustrophobic. It's dark. I'm not supposed to carry a weapon. It's loud. I can't hear if someone's sneaking up behind me, and it's a shame because I do love a good movie with a huge tub of popcorn dripping in butter, and a great big Coke."

"No Junior Mints?"

This was what made Blake Harrison appealing. She'd bared her soul, and instead of digging deeper into the stories she wasn't ready to tell, he decided to quiz her on her choice of movie candy. He made it difficult for her to keep her perspective. "Sour Patch Kids."

"Right."

Something caught her eye. What was that? She rushed to the opposite window, waved Blake over. "There he is. That door, two over. Where does it go?"

"It's a back entrance to the warehouse."

"He's been in the warehouse this whole time? What's he been doing?"

"I don't know."

Why had he been in the warehouse? She'd have to spend

some more time in there next week. Maybe he'd hidden something.

She turned to Blake. "Guess it's safe for us to get back to work. Sorry for keeping you cooped up in here."

"No problem."

He held the door for her. As she passed him, he touched her elbow. The tingle that shot through her arm made no sense at all and she paused.

"Thanks," he said in a husky whisper. "It's nice to get to know you better."

The wistfulness in his words made her wonder if maybe friendships were a rare commodity in his world, as well. But why would that be? A guy like Blake Harrison shouldn't have any trouble making friends. But maybe he did. Maybe his work and home life left little room for outside relationships. The insight surprised her and made her want to reach out to him even more than before. "I hope you understand… It's a fine line, the one I'm walking, being me, but not me. I don't have the luxury of opening up with everyone, but when it's you and me, it will be the real me."

"Fair enough."

Why had she said that? He might want friends, but she wasn't the kind he needed. Better try to warn him off. "You might not like the real me." There was no "might." He wouldn't. The real Heidi was scarred and damaged and broken. No one wanted to deal with that.

Two days later, Blake eased into his porch swing and set his mug of decaf in the cup holder built into the arm. He tapped the news icon on his iPad and scrolled through the latest reports. Typical Sunday night.

Yeah, right. He couldn't even kid himself. His usual Sunday evening routine included a little ESPN, maybe a few tech magazines or an episode of *Doctor Who*.

In the days since Heidi's arrival, he'd become obses-

sive about checking national and international news. Not
that he knew what he was looking for. Some clue, some
hidden report about a crime family, something that might
jump out at him and tell him why Mark Hammond—he
still couldn't think of him as Markos Kovac—had chosen
to move to North Carolina. But the reports contained the
usual celebrity scandals, political gaffes and a scathing
opinion piece on how badly the meteorologists bumbled
the hurricane season predictions.

Nothing to indicate the end of the world lurked over
the horizon.

He peered through the trees at the cabin where Heidi
was staying. Light flickered between the plantation blinds
Caroline had installed to replace the crumbling miniblinds
that had graced the windows since the mid-'80s.

Heidi had requested permission to install what she'd
called "a few security measures" in the cabin and the surrounding property, but as far as he could tell, she'd set up
housekeeping with nothing more than two suitcases and
a laptop.

He didn't know the specifics of what security measures
she planned to put in place. He assumed it involved cameras, listening devices, maybe a few caches of weapons.
Sooner or later, she'd have to haul stuff in and if she followed the TV script for this crime drama she was starring
in, he'd expect her to do it at night.

He took a sip of coffee. Cold. He could pour a hot cup,
but what if he missed—

Good grief. He was turning into a stalker. He grabbed
the cup and yanked the screen door open. He forced himself to take his time, dumping out the coffee, filling the
cup, stirring in some cream. He even took a few minutes
to check on Maggie and adjust the comforter away from
her face.

There. He checked his watch. Eleven-fifteen. He'd taken

a full ten minutes away from staring at a house where an undercover FBI agent had probably turned in three hours ago and forgotten to turn off the lights. Or maybe she didn't like the dark. With what she'd seen, he could understand that.

He shook his head. *Lord, I'm losing it here.*

He held the door as it closed to prevent it from slamming into the door frame, and turned back to the swing. He'd sit here, drink his coffee, and when he'd finished it he would go to bed. Nothing weird about that.

The sound of a door scraping along the wood floor of the cabin porch startled him. Coffee sloshed over his hand and onto his jeans. He sat straighter and focused on the sound. No one had knocked. No one had driven into the narrow driveway. So who was walking into the cabin?

The door opened and closed, then the storm door closed on its own. Multiple shadows appeared in the windows. Neither of them looked to be Heidi's. He'd noticed it last night, how her hair cast a shadow around her head. One of the figures had her general build, but not her hair. The other was a man. Tall, broad shoulders.

Stalker, stalker, stalker… The words reverberated in his mind. This was stupid. What kind of idiot watched the house of a secret agent at midnight? Even if she ran into trouble, what did he think he could do other than get in her way? She was more than capable of taking care of herself. What she was doing over there was none of his business. She'd told him she wouldn't be working alone. Whoever these people were, they had to be on her side. On his side.

He sat frozen with indecision. They had to be friends of hers, but…what if they weren't? What if she was in trouble?

Okay. Not likely. But…

He reached for his phone. Found the number. Hit Send. Two rings. Three.

"Blake?"

He'd surprised her. "Um, hey." Brilliant. He was sure to convince her of his mental stability with that one.

"Is everything all right?"

"I wanted to ask you the same question. I'm not trying to be nosy, but I heard your door open a few minutes ago. Wanted to be sure you were all right." That was better.

Heidi's laughter floated on the air. "Blake, do you mind if I come over for a second?"

Come over? At midnight?

"Yes. I mean, no. No, I don't mind. Come on over."

The call ended and the door of the cabin opened. Two figures emerged and approached. Was one of them Heidi?

He walked down the path to meet them. He stopped at the edge of his yard and waited. In the moonlight, they were hard to see. When they reached him, he understood why.

"You look like a cat burglar," he blurted out. In skintight black clothes, her hair pulled up in a tight bun and with her face covered in black paint, Heidi could have walked within a few feet of him and he'd have missed her.

Her companion laughed. "An accurate description." He stuck out a blackened hand. "Max Jacobs. Pleasure to meet you."

Blake shook the hand, noting the firm grip, the hint of a challenge in the squeeze. This guy meant business.

Heidi grinned, her teeth shining bright in her darkened face. "Max is my partner. I wanted you to meet so if you see him around, you'll know he's one of the good guys."

Max snickered. "Even if I do look like a criminal."

Heidi's partner was a man. He shouldn't be surprised. He'd guess most undercover FBI agents were men. Still. He didn't like it.

Not that it was any of his business. And one thing was for sure, if Heidi landed in some kind of trouble, this guy looked like he could handle himself and anyone who tried to mess with her. There was some comfort in that.

"Mr. Harrison—" Max said.

"Please, call me Blake."

Max nodded. "Okay, Blake. Listen, man, I know she rolled up in here and dropped a bomb on you. If you need to talk, want to ask questions, we get that. Your little girl has stolen the heart of every agent on this team. We'll protect her with our lives. You and your family are doing an incredible thing here and we appreciate it."

Blake nodded as he tried to come up with something to say. "Thank you" seemed inadequate, although he meant it. "I don't think I'm doing anything incredible, but I do hope you'll pass my gratitude on to the rest of the agents. My daughter, and my entire family's safety, is my greatest concern and I—I'll rest easier knowing you guys are looking out for them."

"I get that, man." Max turned to Heidi. "I'm gonna check in with the team before I turn in."

Max blended back into the night and Heidi watched him go until the door opened and closed again. Then she turned back to Blake. "That's Max."

"Seems like a great guy."

"Yeah. He is."

"Y'all are close?"

"Like siblings. We fight like you and Caroline, make up quick. Would kill anyone who messed with the other."

Most people meant that figuratively. In her case, it was probably literal.

"I have to turn in, as well. I hear my new boss is a stickler for promptness."

"I've heard that, too."

She backed up a few steps. "He's a good guy, calling to check on me and make sure I wasn't being attacked by strangers. Impressive."

She jogged toward the cabin.

"Good night, Blake." The words floated back to him. Seconds later, the dead bolt slid home on her door.

She didn't think he'd overreacted. She knew he'd been checking on her and she was impressed.

Not that it mattered what she thought.

EIGHT

Monday morning blared into Heidi's consciousness with a phone ringing well before daylight. She rolled over and fought her eyelids' desperate attempts to slam shut as her hands searched the pillow for her phone.

"Zimmerman," she said.

"Sorry to wake you, Z. It's Richards."

She'd worked with Kyle Richards for a few months when she did TacOps early in her career and knowing he was running the surveillance side of this case helped her sleep at night.

Except when it didn't. "What is it?"

"Got something, might be nothing."

"Let's hear it."

"One of the heat signatures in the Kovac house disappeared."

That woke her up. "What?"

"We've had two heat signatures since Kovac came home last night. Now we have one."

"Did he go outside to smoke?"

"It didn't move, Z. It's gone."

"You ever seen anything like this before?"

"A few times. I'm guessing there's either an underground room or a panic room."

"Is this the first time we've noticed it here?" Heidi did a

few air squats to try to get some blood pumping. The clock said it was too late to go back to sleep.

"Yep, but that doesn't mean it's the first time it's happened. We don't have the manpower or equipment to check for heat signatures all the time. We spot-check. Happened to have the equipment on when one of them up and disappeared. Freaked Jillson out." Richards snorted and Heidi heard a distant "Did not!" through the phone.

"We'll keep checking for it to reappear and will let you know when it does."

"I assume looking for this room will be a priority Friday night?"

TacOps could study a suspect and their routines for as long as ten weeks before planning a home visit. But Katarina Kovac had made dinner reservations in Asheville and the TacOps team was confident the Kovacs would be away from home for at least three hours on Friday evening. Not as much time as they'd need, but it would be a start.

"You got it."

She yawned.

Richards chuckled. "Sorry about waking you up, but I thought you should know we're on alert over here. In case something goes down—"

"No apologies. It's what I want you to do."

"That's why I like you, Z. You're one of the few agents who don't cuss me out when I call them this early."

"I try to keep my malevolent thoughts to myself," she said.

"Whatever, but listen." Richards paused and his voice lost the teasing tone. "You need to be careful. I don't know what's going on, but I've done this a long time, and people who act like these folks are not normal."

"No one is normal."

"I know, but these people are nowhere near it. I'm serious, Z. I have a feeling about this one and I'm rarely wrong. Keep your head in the game. We've got a live one over here."

Heidi was still thinking about Richard's comment as she walked into her office three hours later. Nothing about this case had gone as anticipated. After two attempts—maybe a third, if the stroke really hadn't been from natural causes—in as many days, all had been quiet for a solid week. It made no sense. What kind of moron criminal tipped his hand before he was ready to act? And why target Blake or Caroline Harrison?

She sat at her desk and scanned her calendar. Today she'd be paying a visit to the company that provided the small chips HPI melted and extruded into custom containers. She and Blake were leaving at 9:00 a.m. and should be back in time for the afternoon meeting.

A whole day alone with Blake Harrison.

This should be interesting.

They got in the car, she with a cup of tea she'd brewed a few minutes earlier, he with a bottle of Mountain Dew. The company had Coke machines in the break area, but Blake Harrison had a small fridge in his office stocked with nothing but Mountain Dew.

"What's with the Mountain Dew?" Not the most important question on her mind, but it was driving her nuts.

"What's with the tea?" He rolled his eyes. "You brew the stuff in your office from your own special little pot and your special-ordered loose tea. You have some nerve to mock my Dew."

"I'm not mocking it." She'd ignore the fact that he'd just mocked her tea. For now. "I'm asking."

"You first," he said.

"Fine." She'd accept the challenge. "Tea bags are gross."

"What?"

"Don't get me wrong, I enjoy sweet iced tea, and I realize it's usually brewed from bags, but let's face it, the sugar covers up most of the tea-bag taste. When I'm drinking my tea hot, I want to taste tea, not paper."

"You can taste paper?"

"You can't?"

He shook his head. Maybe he'd realized the futility of arguing with her on this point.

"Where'd you learn to drink tea?"

"My roommate in college, Sara. Her mom is British. She grew up having tea every afternoon. It rubbed off on me. Then I went to England one summer with her and I claimed the tradition as my own."

"Explains a lot," he said with heavy sarcasm.

"Hey, that's what I am. A weird compilation of all the people who've touched my life. I don't have the family history you have—years of tradition, people who've known me since birth, a family to remind me of how we've always done things. Over the years, I've picked up all sorts of random stuff."

"Like the tea."

"Like the tea."

"And?"

"And what?"

"What else?"

Heidi stared out the window for a while. "New pajamas for Christmas Eve." She blinked back the sudden moisture in her eyes. "There was a family. They were wonderful to me." Why had she brought this up? Why?

"They did new pajamas?" The gentleness in his prompt triggered another rapid round of blinking. That Christmas. The best one she'd ever had. The new pajamas wrapped under the tree. The hoots of laughter as they all went to try them on and then posed for the pictures.

The insistence that she be in the pictures. She could

still hear David Thompson's words. Feel the warmth in his smile. *You're part of the family, Heidi.*

She wondered if he would be proud of the woman she had become. Uncle Frank said he would.

"Heidi?" Blake's worried voice cut through her reverie.

"Yeah, sorry. Memories," she said.

"How many families?"

She knew what he meant. "I lost count. I only remember the ones that were horrible or beautiful. Some of them were too brief to register."

"How did…" Blake's hands flexed on the wheel. "How did you…?"

She knew what he was curious about, even without him asking. "Do you want to know how I wound up in foster care, or how I survived the system without a criminal background?"

"Either? Both?"

This was dangerous territory. Scary. She couldn't tell him everything. The horror, the pain, the confusion, the senseless death. The damage to her sense of self, physically and emotionally. The new face, the new name, the new…everything.

"Sorry," he said. "You don't have to tell me." She glanced at him in time to see the red tinge his neck. Why would he be embarrassed?

"No, it's a fair question. I'm trying to decide how to answer it."

"Trying to think up a slick version?" The teasing in his tone took the sting out of his words.

She swatted his arm. "No. It's complicated and some of it I'm not at liberty to discuss."

"Seriously?"

"Yep."

"Wow."

She blew out a long breath. *Here goes.* "I never knew

my father. He split when I was a baby. My mother, well, I think she tried. Maybe she didn't. I don't really remember her. Regardless, I went into foster care at age eight." She swallowed back the memory of that first night with a strange family. The house was warm and she'd had plenty to eat, but she'd cried herself to sleep wondering what would happen to her mother.

Blake didn't press. She'd have to be very careful about what she said from here on out. He was such a good listener, it would be far too easy to slip up and say more than she intended.

"I was a pretty good kid, but it was hard. Hard to do well in school when you change schools with each new family, hard to even care when college seemed so out of reach. Sometimes a guidance counselor or teacher would see something in me and make an effort, but I'd wind up switching schools and having to prove myself all over again."

She took a sip of her tea. "I wound up in a bad situation." She still had the scar over her eyebrow to remind her of that one. "Someone made a phone call, and next thing I knew, I wound up with a family unlike any I'd ever known. New clothes that fit. My own room. No one yelling. Compassion. Acceptance. They saved my life."

"Wow."

"Yep."

"I'm sure they are proud of you."

Heidi tried to respond, but her throat constricted.

"Heidi?"

"It's okay. I, um, I think they would be. They, uh, they died." She couldn't bring herself to say it had been an accident. There had been nothing accidental about the inferno that took them from her.

"Heidi. I'm sorry."

His hand reached for hers, and for some reason, she allowed him to give it a gentle squeeze. He couldn't have meant it as anything more than comfort, but his touch sent a tingle up her arm and she missed the sensation of his hand on hers as soon as he pulled it away.

"How old were you?"

"Seventeen. I'd only been with them a year. They had planned to adopt me but the adoption never went through. Uncle Frank was the only surviving family member. He put me through college, looked out for me. Saved my life for the second time."

She'd said more than she'd intended. Way more. Time to change the direction of this conversation. "Enough of my drama. Let's talk about something else. What's Caroline's story? No steady boyfriend? No ex-husband? Does she do anything other than work?"

He must have sensed she didn't want to talk about herself anymore and he shifted gears with her. "Caroline dated a guy in college. He died. Hit by a drunk driver."

"No." That hadn't been in her file.

"She had a hard time. Took a semester off. When she went back, she was all about work and family, nothing else. Graduated summa cum laude, came to HPI and took our finances into the modern age." He leaned his head against the headrest and his hands flexed on the steering wheel. "She discovered the discrepancies in the accounting. She came to me one day, trembling, holding a spreadsheet. Told me she'd tried to find an explanation that made sense, but the one that didn't make sense was the only one that fit."

Heidi could only imagine how hard that had been. She'd seen how close Caroline and Blake were. For her to have to tell him his wife had been taking money from the company accounts had to have been excruciating.

"Anyway." He blew out a long breath. "She's amazing, but she works too much and her friends from childhood and from college have all gotten married. Some of them have kids. She feels as if she's already missed out on those opportunities. She doesn't talk about it much, but when she does, she always sounds hopeless. Like she's trapped here. I've told her to look for work somewhere else, take a leave of absence, travel, whatever. Told her she can always come back if she wants, not to feel like she has to stay, but she won't go. And now with Dad…"

Jeffrey Harrison's recovery had been remarkable, but Heidi could see how Caroline would take his health issues to be one more sign that she needed to stay close and focus on the family rather than on herself.

"I'm sure someone will come along and realize what a prize she is." That's how it worked, wasn't it? Not that she would know from personal experience. She had a gift for terrifying men into running for their lives long before she ever had a chance to determine if they were worth hanging around. The only one who'd stayed long enough to see what the Kovacs had done to her had skipped out soon after, confirming her suspicions that there was no point in pursuing relationships. They never worked. At least, not for her.

Not that it mattered. She'd known since the day the Kovacs had scarred her for life that her purpose here was about one thing. Stopping them from ever hurting anyone again the way they'd hurt her.

Anyway, the dating scene had never appealed to her. Why would she waste her time with boys who had no idea how dangerous the world was? She'd spent her college summers learning how to run surveillance and slip in and out of buildings undetected. She'd spent hours mastering Hungarian, years pushing every selfish impulse to the side so she could someday take the Kovacs down.

And that's what she was going to do.

Blake pulled into the parking lot of their largest supplier and cut the engine. He'd been looking forward to having this time with Heidi, and it had been enlightening. He had many more questions, but he could tell when she'd said all she would say and he had enough sense to know pressing her would be counterproductive.

Trying to understand where she'd draw the line on what she would and would not discuss was giving him a headache. Or maybe the headache had already been there. He'd been up late last night, but even his morning Mountain Dew hadn't helped him perk up. Good thing he'd brought another for later.

"Are you okay?" Heidi's eyes narrowed in concern.

"Yeah." No way would he own up to how miserable he felt. Not when he knew she'd been out running around all hours of the night doing who knew what to keep his family safe, and she sat here all bubbly and energetic. He might have to cave and try drinking some of her fancy-pants tea. "I'm good. Let's check this place out. If we get done early enough to beat the rush, I'll take you to a great burger joint a couple of miles from here."

"Sounds good."

They toured the plant, Heidi introducing herself as a quality consultant interested in learning how much variation could be expected in their raw materials. The engineer tasked with giving them the tour looked like he'd graduated a week ago, and it took Heidi less than three seconds to wrap him around her little finger. Poor boy didn't know what had hit him.

They finished in plenty of time and when they walked back to the car, Heidi held her hand out. "Why don't you let me drive?"

"Why?"

"You look awful."

He opened the passenger door for her. "Thanks a lot."

She climbed in. When he slid into the driver's seat she made a show of buckling her seat belt. "Maybe *awful*'s the wrong word. You look…off. I can't put my finger on it. Is something bothering you?"

"I have a headache." He reached into the cooler he had in the backseat and pulled out another Mountain Dew. His mouth felt as if he'd been snacking on cotton balls. "This should help."

She laughed. "You never did tell me about your obsession with Mountain Dew."

"It's no big thing. We have Coke products at the plant because that's what Dad and Caroline prefer. But there's nothing quite like a Mountain Dew to get your morning off to a great start."

He took a long drink. "A couple of years ago, they gave me the fridge and stocked it with Mountain Dew for my birthday. I keep a few bottles in there all the time."

He took another swallow. "I've cut back over the years. I only drink one a day."

She pursed her lips and eyed the bottle he held in his hand.

"Two in cases of emergency."

She shook her head. "As I recall, you had a Mountain Dew the night I showed up at your house. Your one-a-day rule seems like it might be more of a guideline."

That memory of hers was going to get him in trouble.

"That one was your fault. I think most people would agree that the FBI knocking on your door constitutes an emergency."

She was laughing as he pulled into the restaurant parking lot. He killed the engine and watched for Heidi's reaction. This place was a dive. The kind of spot a tourist wouldn't even notice, unless they bothered to pay attention to the parking lot overflowing with everything from beat-up pickups to shiny luxury sedans.

Heidi looked around and then back at him. "You sure know how to impress a girl." Amusement shone from her eyes. He'd picked this place on purpose. Partly because he loved the food and made it a point to eat here whenever he came to town, but also because he wanted to see how she would react. He'd learned a long time ago that the best way to get to know someone was to take them out of their comfort zone. The way people treat others who are different from them was a solid indicator of their character.

He hadn't paid it much attention when he was dating Lana, but later he'd noticed how she mocked others for things as simple as what type of music they enjoyed or where they shopped. He was convinced it was her lack of respect for others that had allowed her to make the decisions that led to her choice to embezzle the money. She could have told him the truth. Told him about the drug addiction. He would have helped her. Five years later, and he still didn't know what he'd done wrong.

Shaking off the memories didn't prove as difficult as it usually was. When he was with Heidi, and even when he wasn't, she took up all available brain space. As they sat down to lunch, her face glowed with obvious delight over the crowded picnic-style tables, the no-nonsense waitress, the cross-section of society represented. He'd have enjoyed her reaction more if he hadn't been counting the minutes until he could go home and lie down.

They ate their cheeseburgers and hand-cut fries, while he gulped three glasses of tea. She chatted with the people around them and kept him from having to do anything more than focus on breathing, chewing and swallowing. He didn't argue when she popped her last bite into her mouth and suggested they leave. He agreed on the pretense that they should free up the table space for the people waiting to get in before the food ran out.

But the truth was, he was feeling so sick he thought he might collapse.

She reached for the keys when they got outside. "You have to let me drive."

He hesitated. He didn't want to admit how wretched he felt. His head throbbed and once during lunch, he'd thought there were two of her sitting across from him. "Fine."

He slid into the passenger seat and closed his eyes. Heidi cranked the car and drove them straight to the interstate without asking for directions even once. "How did you do that?"

"Do what?"

"Remember how to get to the interstate."

"I paid attention on the way here. It's never a good idea to drive off into the boonies and not have a handle on how to get back to civilization."

Made sense. In a weird, creepy way. "Do you ever relax?"

"No."

She laughed, but Blake had a feeling she wasn't kidding. He tried to swallow. Why was his mouth dry? This was embarrassing. Spend the day with the FBI agent and instead of being witty and impressing her with his skill and knowledge, he could barely hold his head up. He tapped the button to lower the temperature on his side of the car.

"Are you hot?" Heidi asked.

"You aren't?"

"No."

Were they going faster? She should slow down. She'd get a ticket. Or would she? Did FBI agents get tickets? Maybe she had some special Get Out of Jail pass in her wallet.

Why was she yelling? Was she yelling at him? Or someone else?

He wanted to ask her what was wrong, but his tongue refused to cooperate. He should tell her he thought he might be having a heart attack. Nothing was working right. What was happening to him?

NINE

Heidi paced the emergency room, thankful she shared it with no one but a young family waiting with their eight year-old sporting a black eye and a broken nose. She gathered the boy had been in a fight and his fellow combatant had already been taken back with more significant injuries.

The boy was explaining his side of the story to his father, complete with sound effects, when her phone rang. Max.

"What's the status?"

"They have no idea at the moment, but I suspect atropine poisoning."

"What?"

"He has classic symptoms. Flushed skin. Dry mouth. Got a little loopy on me. Mumbled something about having a heart attack. When I got him in here, his pulse was sky-high."

"Let me guess, you read about this once when you were twelve."

"Twenty-three. In a manual you should have read, too, on different poisons and drugs and their side effects."

"Not all of us remember everything we've ever read."

She ignored his sarcasm.

"Why do you think someone tried to poison him?"

"I don't know. It's ridiculous. I can't even figure out how the poison was administered. Maybe I'm wrong about the atropine. I'm hoping we can chalk it up to stress. Or maybe even too much caffeine." He did consume a lot of caffeine. "Something weird is going on. If he'd been driving..."

She didn't want to think about it.

"This is twice in less than two weeks."

"I know."

"Why now?"

"I don't know."

A nurse poked her head through the door. "Ms. Zimmerman?"

"Yes."

"You can come back."

"Max, I have to go. Call you in a few."

She followed the nurse through the doors. Blake lay still, skin flushed, hooked up to an IV. The nurse nodded in his direction. "We've already done an EKG and he's stable. The doctor will check back in a few minutes after we get some labs back. You can sit with him if you'd like."

Heidi approached the bed and Blake's eyelids fluttered open. "Hey." The word came out as a whisper. He cleared his throat and tried again. "Hey."

"Hey."

"Thank you. Again."

"For what?"

He gave her a withering look. "Please. I'm not an idiot."

She leaned close. "Let's save our debate on that point until after you're home."

His eyes flashed, but he smiled. "Any idea when that will be?"

She shrugged. "I'm not sure if they'll let you go or keep you for observation."

"What do you think they should do?"

Good question. Hanging around hospitals was never fun, but if someone had poisoned him, they'd done it either in his home or office. Home might not be a safe place for him, after all.

"I think you need to rest. When you feel up to it, you need to think through every single thing you've done since yesterday. Everything."

"Why?"

"We'll need to check your house, your office—"

"Wait a minute. What are you thinking?"

"We need to think of something you would have ingested. Only you. So it can't be the coffee at the office or last night's supper."

"You don't think this is a fluke?"

"Do you?"

He shrugged. "I don't know. I heard one of the doctors say it looked like a panic attack."

"You aren't the type to panic."

"How would you know? Maybe I freak out all the time." He kept his tone light, but Heidi could hear the undercurrent. He might need some encouragement.

"I've seen you in a life-or-death situation. You handled it fine. And while it is normal and expected for you to experience some physical ramifications from the stress levels you are operating under—"

"Such as?"

"Upset stomach, headache, tight muscles in your neck and back, short-temper, disturbed sleep." She ticked the list off on her fingers. "All normal."

She tapped the edge of the hospital bed. "Flushed skin, not being able to get enough to drink, feeling dizzy and having a sky-high pulse are indicators you've ingested something that has messed with you in an unpleasant way. And since I've been with you all morning and I feel fine, it has to be something only you have—"

"My Mountain Dew."

"What?"

"I guarantee you it's the Mountain Dew."

"Blake, a sealed bottle of Mountain Dew would be hard to poison."

"Not that hard. I saw it on one of those forensics shows on TV. You stab the top of the cap with a strong syringe and pull the plastic back through. It wouldn't be noticeable."

"You watch too much TV."

Not that the criminals couldn't get their ideas from television, too. He was watching for her reaction. She didn't like it, but it was possible.

"I was fine this morning before I left the office. Things got weird after I drank the first Mountain Dew, and after I finished the second one… I honestly don't remember how I got here." He narrowed his eyes at her. "How did you know to bring me here?"

"It didn't require much in the way of specialized training. Aside from the physical symptoms, you kept saying you could see two of me. Taking you to the hospital seemed like the most prudent course of action."

"Sorry."

"Don't be. I am thankful you let me drive."

She glanced around. The nurse would banish her if she caught her using the cell phone, but this was worth the risk. "Max, I need someone to meet me in the hospital parking lot. I want labs run on Blake's Mountain Dew."

"His what?"

She explained Blake's theory. "He wasn't feeling well this morning, but he got significantly worse after he drank the second one. They came from his personal stash. Everyone at the plant knows he drinks one every morning." Meaning Markos would have known.

"All right. I'll call you when we get there," Max said.

Blake sucked in a deep breath. "I don't like this."

"You deserve an award for your skillful use of understatement."

Blake didn't laugh. "Someone poisoned me, didn't they?"

Heidi held his gaze. He deserved the truth, even if it terrified him. "I don't know, but it looks that way."

It was 7:00 p.m. when Heidi drove up the long Harrison driveway with a grumpy Blake in the seat.

"You'd better go straight to Mom and Dad's," he said. "They will want to see for themselves that I'm okay."

"No problem."

They went inside. Eleanor Harrison grabbed Blake and squeezed him close. "Honey, we were so worried." She turned to Heidi and pulled her in for a hug. Eleanor Harrison was the huggiest woman Heidi had ever encountered. "Thank you for staying with him, dear."

"It was my pleasure." No need to mention that nothing could have forced her to leave.

Eleanor and Jeffrey had taken the news of Markos Kovac's presence far better than she could have hoped for.

For that matter, they'd taken *her* presence far better than she could have hoped for.

Jeffrey had only been home a few hours when Blake and Caroline had filled their parents in on the Kovac situation.

Heidi had planned to fly under the radar as much as possible. She hadn't wanted to cause any more stress than was absolutely necessary.

But Jeffrey and Eleanor had other ideas. Both parents had insisted on meeting her immediately. She'd kept her visit short, but somehow, that had been enough for Eleanor to start treating her like a member of the family.

Jeffrey spent hours each day in therapy and hadn't yet returned to the office, but Blake and Caroline paid him daily visits, both to check on his progress and to share any updates on the case.

Heidi had seen stress pull more than one family apart,

but in the face of crisis, the Harrisons seemed to be growing closer by the hour.

And pulling her along with them.

"You'd better go speak to your father, dear," Eleanor said to Blake. "Since he heard you were in the hospital, he's been as skittish as a cat on a porch full of rocking chairs." She clucked her tongue and went into the kitchen. "You'll stay for dinner, won't you, Heidi? Caroline took Maggie to basketball practice but they should be here any minute. I know Maggie will want to see you."

"Thank you, ma'am, but I should—"

"Nonsense. You need some decent food. I hear you live on ham sandwiches." She gave her a look indicating her extreme disapproval of Heidi's nutritional choices. "I've been cooking since we got home from the doctor and there's a gracious plenty."

The house did smell amazing. Her grumbling stomach sealed the deal. Another hour of hanging out with the Harrisons wouldn't hurt anything. She texted Max to let him know her plans and then settled onto a bar stool as Eleanor Harrison rolled out a batch of homemade biscuits.

Blake tapped on his dad's bedroom door.

"Come in," Jeffrey said.

Blake pushed the door open and found his dad sitting in one of two recliners in the sitting area of the massive bedroom. His face broke into a huge smile when he saw Blake. "You're okay?"

Blake gave him a hug and then flopped in the other chair. "I'm fine, Dad."

He could tell his dad didn't fully buy it, but he hadn't decided what he should share. He and Heidi had gone back and forth about it the whole drive home. No evidence had indicated his dad's stroke had been anything other than a tragic natural event, and his recovery continued to be swift and remarkable.

Still, he hated to burden him with the knowledge that someone had tried to poison him today.

And it had been poison. The only time Heidi had left his side had been for the ten minutes when she'd raced to the parking lot to give Max the almost-empty bottle of Mountain Dew from the cup holder of his car. How they'd managed to test it in one afternoon he'd never know, but thirty minutes before he was discharged, Heidi's phone had lit up with one word.

Atropine.

Blake now knew more than he'd ever wanted to know about atropine. He'd especially loved the part where Heidi had told him if he'd downed the Mountain Dew more quickly, or had the second one immediately after the first, the results could have been fatal.

Heidi planned to go to his office later tonight, remove all the bottles of Mountain Dew in his fridge and have them checked, as well. She expected to find them all laced with atropine.

Heidi didn't know if they'd been trying to kill him outright, or if the goal had been to incapacitate him. Either way, someone was out to get him. The obvious someone was Mark.

"Let's hear it." His dad spoke with authority, and Blake knew trying to sugarcoat the situation wouldn't work.

"Looks like someone's trying to kill me, Dad." Saying the words aloud, watching the emotions race across his dad's face, made it all so real, but he didn't want his dad to see how worried he was. He blew out a long breath. "Heidi's staying close, and she's recommended I switch to water."

His dad smiled. "I'm proud of you, son."

Blake gulped. Even at thirty-three, his dad's approval

meant everything. Although in this case, he didn't think he deserved it.

"We will get through this. You stick close to Heidi and do what she says. I know she looks like a fragile little thing, but from what they told me, she's brilliant and lethal. I have a lot of questions about this stuff, but one thing I know for sure. We are safer with her here."

What? "Who told you that?" Had he talked to Max? Or one of the other agents?

His dad winked. "You didn't think I was going to sit here and twiddle my thumbs, did you? I know a few people who know a few people."

"Dad, I don't know if digging around into Heidi's background is a good idea." Heidi had told him how compartmentalized everything had to be, for her protection and to keep from spooking the Kovacs.

His dad didn't look worried. "We've never talked much about what I did in Vietnam, I guess."

"No." Never.

"We aren't going to start now, but it happens that a buddy of mine from back then is a bigwig at the FBI. I made a call. He paid me a visit. We talked."

A rush of emotion squeezed Blake's chest. His dad was always looking out for them, even while recovering from a stroke.

"I know she made a good case, but I wanted to be sure. And I am. She's the real deal. And you made the right call. I've assured him she'll get our full support."

He cleared his throat. "He asked if I wanted to receive regular updates from Heidi, but I told him no. Told him my son had things well in hand."

Blake swallowed hard.

"I don't know why I've been sidelined, son." Jeffrey tapped his recliner and shook his head ruefully. "But while my body may not be cooperating with me, my brain is hard at work. I'm praying for you, for Heidi. Even for Mark. All day. I wonder if that's why I'm here, because God knew the best way for me to fight this battle was from my knees."

Blake stared at his dad in amazement. He could only hope he would be like him someday. "Thanks, Dad."

"Let's pray before we go eat that delicious dinner your mom's been working on all afternoon."

His dad had been praying over him for as long as he could remember and Blake had always known it. But as he listened to his father plead for protection and wisdom, for him and for Heidi, and even for Mark to turn his heart to God, Blake thought his own heart might explode.

He walked into the kitchen more confident than he'd been since the moment Heidi had jumped into his car eleven days ago. Maybe God hadn't dropped the ball after all. Maybe God had been moving the pieces into the best position possible.

His mom flipped over chicken in the cast-iron skillet. "Grab me that plate, dear." She nodded toward a platter lined with paper towels and he slid it to her.

"Where's Heidi?" Had she gone while he'd been upstairs with his dad?

"She's in the dining room. Why don't you take her those napkins?"

Blake did as he was told and found Heidi walking around the dining room table with a hand full of knives and forks. "Mom said you needed these."

She grinned. "Thanks."

He followed her around the table, folding napkins and sliding them under the forks. "Mom put you to work, huh?"

"She volunteered!" his mom called from the kitchen.

Heidi scrunched up her cute little nose and grinned. "I like your mom," she said in a whisper.

"She likes you, too," he whispered back.

Maggie burst through the door. "Daddy!" She ran

straight for him and he swung her around. Everyone had agreed Maggie did not need to know about his trip to the ER. She'd become clingy since his car "accident" and no one wanted to add any more worry to her world.

After a few moments of cuddles, she dashed to Heidi and didn't leave her side. Heidi didn't seem to mind her little shadow.

Caroline arrived as they took their seats and as his father asked the blessing, Blake glanced around the table. Heidi sat across from him and somehow, her presence made their family circle feel more whole than it had in a long time.

By the time dinner ended, his mom had secured a promise from Heidi that she would celebrate Thanksgiving with them and even though he knew it was crazy, he liked the idea of spending more time with her outside the office.

He walked her home an hour later, and when Maggie ran along ahead of them, she nudged his arm with her elbow.

"Are you sure you're okay with me being around on Thanksgiving? Your mom's invitation caught me off guard, but I can come up with an excuse..."

His stomach flipped. "I don't mind, but I hate to take you away from—" He ran out of words. Did she have anyone to spend the holiday with? He scrambled to come up with someone. "Uncle Frank? Maybe Max? Or your boyfriend?" He held his breath.

"Uncle Frank and Aunt Ginny usually travel to Florida over Thanksgiving, so if I'm not working, I spend the day with Sara. If I am working, I spend it with Max."

"Sara is your college roommate?"

She smiled. "Yes."

"So there's Max and Sara—"

She laughed.

"What?"

"You're nosy tonight. I'm going to have to add this symptom to the list of effects from atropine poisoning."

"Sorry."

"No, you aren't." She laughed again. "The answer to the question you're trying to ask is no. I don't have a boyfriend. Haven't in a long time. Something about my charming personality repels men. Or maybe it's my electric-socket hair."

"I'm never going to live that down, am I?"

She grinned and shook her head, but then the smile left her face. "This job doesn't lend itself to relationships. Too much time away, too much baggage, too many scars." She took in a long breath and blew it out.

"As for the other question you aren't asking, Max and I were teamed up straight off the Farm and have worked together ever since. We hit it off immediately, but never in a romantic way. He's the brother I always wanted."

He didn't bother to pretend he hadn't been curious. He almost pointed out that Max needed to have his head examined if he'd truly never considered asking her out, but caught himself. Time to switch gears.

"What does Sara do?"

"She's a psychologist. Specializes in PTSD and works as a consultant for the Bureau and other agencies." She left out the part about how having a roommate with PTSD had helped Sara choose her specialty, or how often she called her friend for an unofficial consultation.

She shook off the serious direction of her thoughts and grinned at Blake. "Anything else you want to know while you can blame it on an overdose?"

He wanted to know more about her, but he needed to remember the promise he'd made to himself after Lana. His first priority was to protect Maggie, even if it meant giving up something he wanted. Besides, if he was reading her correctly, Heidi Zimmerman had no interest in having a relationship with anyone. Certainly not him.

He decided to pull the conversation back to the issue

at hand. The one he woke up thinking about and went to bed praying about. "Do you think he's going to kill me?"

Heidi grabbed his arm and pulled them both to a stop. "You listen to me, Blake Harrison. I don't know why he's trying to hurt you, but I'm not going to sit back and let him have you. We will figure this out. He's going to mess up and when he does, we'll nail his sorry hide. I know we haven't known each other long, but you have my word. I will not rest until we've caught him."

TEN

As far as Blake could tell, Heidi never rested. The night of the atropine poisoning, she'd left his parents and gone to HPI to recover the remaining Mountain Dew bottle from his fridge, and the lights hadn't come back on in the cabin until after midnight. For the rest of the week, she was gone until at least 10:00 p.m. every night. She told him she spent some of her time at the house the FBI had rented for the rest of her team, but he doubted she was napping there. He had no idea when she'd come home on Saturday night. All he knew was that the plan to enter Mark's home had fallen through. The team had been ready to go, but Mark and Katarina had never left the house. Then, despite the fact that he suspected she'd gotten no sleep, she'd gone to church with them on Sunday.

No trace of fatigue lined her face when he saw her on Monday morning. At 10:00 a.m. she made a presentation to him and the entire engineering staff where she outlined the changes she wanted to make to their quality control procedures. It was an impressive accomplishment for a "consultant" who'd only been on-site for two weeks. It was downright astonishing considering her extracurricular activities.

He didn't know how she worked two jobs and stayed

sane, but he was grateful they had a four-day weekend ahead of them. He prayed it would be a calm one.

The Thanksgiving holiday passed uneventfully. Well, if you count having an undercover FBI agent join you for turkey, dressing and skeet shooting while you recover from poisoning as uneventful.

When the family was around, Heidi was a good, but not great shot. She appeared comfortable with the weapons, but was quick to give the others a turn. He almost asked her about it, but she silenced his question with a nod in Maggie's direction.

Ah. Little eyes and ears that saw and heard everything. The last thing they needed was Maggie going to school and telling everyone Heidi was good with a gun.

When his mom took Maggie back to the house, Caroline and his dad went with them. That's when Heidi started showing off. After a few minutes of impressive marksmanship, she'd given him some tips. To his surprise, she made an excellent teacher. He ended the afternoon with a few shots he'd never imagined he could make and Heidi grinned like a proud parent at a spelling bee.

She promised to give him lessons with a handgun later and Blake planned to hold her to it.

The Monday after Thanksgiving, Blake opened his office fridge out of habit and found two bottles of Mountain Dew.

He poked his head into Heidi's office. She pulled the sleeve of her shirt over her elbow as she looked up. She did that a lot. He'd noticed because Caroline never left her shirtsleeves down, she always shoved them up on her arms.

Heidi seemed to want to keep as much of her skin covered as possible. Scarves, long sleeves, pants. Was it to hide her weapons?

He eased into her office and took a seat in front of her

desk. He leaned forward and kept his voice low. "I need to ask you a question."

Her brow furrowed. "Go ahead."

"Do you have any idea who put the Mountain Dew in my fridge?"

She grinned. "I did. I brought them from my fridge this morning. I feel confident they are safe. Well, as safe as any yellow carbonated beverage can be."

"Wow. Thanks."

"You're welcome."

He hopped up and ran back to his office, grabbed the Mountain Dew and returned to the chair in front of her desk. He took a long drink and then got down to business.

"There's something else I need to talk to you about."

"Okay."

"We have an annual Christmas party." He waited for it. Yep. She took in a slow breath, set down the paper she'd been studying and leaned back in her chair. He'd had a feeling she wouldn't like this idea.

"Mom insists we have it this year. Dad's doing great, and she wants everyone to carry on as normal. She thinks it would look suspicious to cancel it."

Heidi dropped her head against her chair and groaned. "I love your mom, but she's going to be the death of me." She shook her head a few times and sat forward. "Tell me about this party."

"It's at Mom and Dad's house."

She rolled her eyes.

"Inside and outside."

She dropped her face into her hands.

"Food, presents, live music."

She pretended to bang her head on her desk.

"We have a huge bonfire, roast marshmallows, sit outside on logs and drink hot chocolate…"

Heidi hadn't lifted her head off her desk.

"The entire HPI family is invited. Some people have other parties to go to and they stop in early or late. Some will be there all night. There are kids running around everywhere…"

Heidi sat up and he couldn't get a read on her expression, but he knew she was not happy. "Did you try to talk her out of it? Did your dad?"

"Yes. But Mom—"

She lifted her hands in mock surrender. "I know."

He didn't say anything else as he watched Heidi process this news.

"How have I not heard about this yet? I would think this would be on everyone's calendar way in advance."

"It is. It has been. I think everyone assumed it would depend on dad's health."

She shoved the stack of papers she'd been working on to the side and pulled out a clipboard with a legal pad stuck on it. "I need every detail you can give me."

For the next hour they talked about everything he knew about the party. The name of the caterers, the band, the party rental store, even where they got the gifts.

"This is not going to be easy." She tapped the pen on the diagram she'd drawn of the house and yard. She'd even included stick figures.

"If you can think of a way we can convince my mother to cancel it, I assure you we'd be fine with that. Well, Mom wouldn't, but she'd survive."

"It's okay."

But it wasn't. He could tell from the shuttered flatness of her eyes, the tension in her shoulders, even the way she took in one long deep breath after another. She didn't like this. And he got the strange sense that there was more behind it than the nightmare security would be for that kind of event.

She gave him a quick smile. "Let me talk to my team. We'll see what we can do."

* * *

Two weeks later, Heidi stood at the edge of the woods behind the Harrisons' home. She'd managed to avoid going outside most of the evening, trusting her team to handle the party out there.

But she didn't have a choice now. Maggie Harrison had begged and pleaded for her to roast marshmallows, and she'd run out of excuses. She held her stick and tried to smile for Maggie as she crammed marshmallows on the end.

"Come on, Miss Heidi."

Blake stood on the other side of the fire talking to none other than Markos Kovac. A group of kids stood nearby licking marshmallow and melted chocolate off their hands as they devoured their s'mores.

Giving TacOps another opportunity to get into the Kovacs' house had been the deciding factor in allowing the party to go on. To everyone's disappointment, Katarina Kovac hadn't attended the party tonight.

Blake had promised to ask Markos about Katarina, and Heidi couldn't decide what she wanted to do more, hear their conversation or keep Maggie as far away from Markos Kovac as possible. She decided on the latter. Blake had an excellent memory and he'd fill her in on what they'd discussed later.

They approached the bonfire and it took every ounce of willpower Heidi had to keep putting one foot in front of the other. When the heat began to warm her face, she paused.

"You can do it, Z," Max said in her ear.

Heidi rubbed her lips together. It was a bonfire. A simple, safe, controlled bonfire. This morning's showers had left the surrounding area soggy and they'd had to work hard to get the flames going in the first place. If a stray spark managed to escape, ten fire extinguishers encircled the area.

No one was in any danger here, certainly not her.

She let Maggie take the lead. "Haven't you ever made s'mores, Miss Heidi?" Concern wrinkled Maggie's face.

Heidi tried to hide the fear flickering through her veins. "It's been a while, Maggie. Why don't you show me your technique?"

Maggie accepted her response and explained how she liked her marshmallows toasted to a light brown, but if they weren't hot enough, they wouldn't melt the chocolate right so it was important to heat them slowly. She sounded so much like Blake when she talked and Heidi's eyes sought him out across the fire.

He was still talking to Markos, but he was watching Maggie. Or was he watching her?

"Looking good, Z." Her team knew she avoided fire, but only Max knew the whole story and he alone understood how hard this night would be. Maggie kept her marshmallows over the hot coals at the edge of the flame, which helped Heidi keep a decent distance from the fire.

As soon as their marshmallows reached the appropriate level of toastiness, she led Maggie to the table where graham crackers and chocolate candy bars waited. Once they constructed their s'mores, they walked toward Blake, Heidi keeping as much distance as she could manage between herself and the fire.

Markos Kovac walked away as they approached. Blake winked at Heidi as Maggie ran toward him, holding out the s'more she'd made for him. "Here, Daddy!"

"Mmm." He chewed for a few moments. "You nailed it!" He gave Maggie a high five.

"I'm gonna see if Papa wants me to make him one." She ran toward Jeffrey, leaving Heidi and Blake munching on their treats.

The wind shifted and blew smoke over them. Heidi

blinked hard as her eyes watered. She forced herself not to run.

"You okay?" he asked.

"Yeah," she lied. "I'm going to walk around and then check on things inside."

Blake frowned. "It's turned into a nice evening. Sure you don't want to stay out here?"

Heidi coughed in the smoke. "Duty calls." She tried to look disappointed as she put more distance between herself and the flames.

"Wait." Blake jogged to where she stood. "I'll come with you."

"No, you stay out here, enjoy the party. I want to hear all about it later," she said with a nod toward Markos Kovac.

"Why don't we walk toward the creek and I'll tell you about it now?" He held out his arm.

Bad idea. Bad idea. Bad idea.

So why did her hand rest in the crook of his arm as he led her deeper into the forest? She took in some deep breaths. She could still smell the smoke, but the fresh air under the canopy of trees helped ease the tightness in her chest.

When they reached the creek, Blake turned to her. "You want to tell me what's going on?"

"What are you talking about?"

"You're skittish. I've never seen you rattled. What aren't you telling me?"

"Sorry, Z," Max said through the earpiece. "You're on your own. I'll check back in later."

She gulped. How was she supposed to handle this? "There's nothing." She shrugged and tried to laugh off his concern.

"I'm not buying it." Blake stood with his arms crossed and even in the moonlight, she saw the worry lining his features. "Don't try to protect me, Heidi Zimmerman. I'm past pretending everything is hunky-dory. If my family's in danger—"

She put her hand out to stop the escalating tirade. "There's nothing going on related to this—" She caught herself. The reason for her fear had everything to do with the Kovac family. Saying it wasn't related to this case wasn't true. Her past was the whole reason she was on this case.

"You promised," he said, his tone censuring her. "How can you expect me to trust you when you won't tell me what's going on?"

He didn't trust her? A lonely ache sizzled around the edges of her heart, but she forced it back. Why should she care what he thought? He had no idea how hard this night had been for her. None. And yet he stood there, demanding an explanation? No. Not this time. "It's personal."

She might as well have slapped him.

He backed away. "I'm sorry I pried." His tone could have frozen lava. He stalked off, back to the party, leaving her standing by the creek. Alone.

What should she have said? That spending weeks in a burn unit will make a person skittish around open flame? That if he'd had half of his body broiled, he wouldn't be a fan of bonfires, either? That the scars on her body, as horrible as they were, didn't compare to the scars seared into her psyche?

Or that the man responsible was the same one Markos Kovac called Uncle?

No. Better he didn't know. Their friendship had been drifting toward something that could never be.

Better if it ended now, before anyone got hurt.

Although the pain scorching her heart told her it might be too late.

ELEVEN

One Month Later

Heidi tossed the file on the coffee table and fell into her favorite chair. She pulled the earpiece from her ear and dropped it on top of the file.

Max flopped onto the sofa. "How are you doing this? There is no way I could get up in three hours and work a full day."

"I don't have a choice. I know it's here, Max. I know it. I haven't found it yet, but there's something here."

"Where else is there to look?"

He had a good point. She knew the process at HPI better than most of the people who worked there. She was on a first-name basis with their raw material suppliers and all their regular customers.

She knew every employee far better than they would like. She knew whose marriages were failing, whose credit was overdrawn, whose kids were on drugs and even whose cancer diagnosis was about to become public knowledge.

But she still didn't know what Markos was after, or why he was targeting the Harrison family.

"We need some time in the house."

TacOps had hoped to get in while the Kovacs visited family over the Christmas holiday, but two burly men appeared at the house ten minutes before the Kovacs left for the airport. At least one of them remained in the house the entire time.

Max groaned. "I know. Last I heard, Richards is working up a plan to stage a chemical spill or something and force an evacuation."

Heidi hated the idea, but she didn't have a better one.

Max kicked off his shoes. They sat in silence for a few minutes. "Z, I have to ask."

She didn't open her eyes. "What?"

"Do you need a break?"

The concern in his voice was genuine and she didn't blame him for asking. She'd have done the same. "Not yet."

"You've been here for ten weeks."

"I spent two weeks in New York last month."

"Following the Kovacs as they traipsed all over New York State for the holidays isn't what I'd call a break. I'm worried about you."

"This isn't my longest undercover assignment. Not even close."

"That doesn't mean you don't need a few days to relax. I can keep an eye on things—"

"No."

"Why not? It's easy enough to justify to everyone at HPI without blowing your cover. A family emergency? Or a long-planned vacation? We can get you out for a few days without anyone being suspicious."

"Not yet."

"Z? You're getting too close to this. To all of it. To the people, the Harrisons. Especially Blake."

"He's trying to help."

"That's not what I mean and you know it."

"I'm a professional, Max." She wished he would drop it. After their disastrous conversation at the Christmas party, she'd expected Blake to keep her at a distance. She'd been shocked when the opposite occurred. She had no idea why, but Blake Harrison seemed to have made it his mission in life to be kind to her. At first, she'd been suspicious. Her training taught her to always suspect an ulterior motive.

But so far, the only thing she'd been able to conclude was that Blake Harrison was one of the most decent men she'd ever had the pleasure to know.

"No one is questioning your professionalism. I'm not just your partner, I'm your other best friend, in case you've forgotten. I see what's happening whether you do or not. He's falling in love with you, and I'm not sure the feeling's not mutual."

"We're just friends."

"For now."

"Forever."

"Famous last words."

Four hours later, Heidi opened her office door. In the center of her desk sat a china saucer with a delicate teacup filled with tea. Still steaming.

She scanned the room before walking to her desk. She dropped her bag into the bottom drawer and turned on her computer before she wrapped her hands around the teacup and inhaled deeply.

One tiny sip confirmed what she'd already known. He'd nailed it. Perfection in a cup. Most people had no idea how to brew a decent cup of tea. Blake hadn't either, but he'd been pestering her since Thanksgiving to show him how she liked it.

A few more sips and she'd be able to face the rest of this crazy day.

The creak of his office chair alerted her to his approach. One, two, three, four steps and the light rat-a-tat on her door followed.

"Come in."

No amount of training or professionalism could have

stopped the smile she knew stretched across her face when he poked his head through the door. "Thank you."

His smile mirrored hers. "Good?"

"Perfect."

He winked and his smile turned smug before fading as he studied her. "Everything okay?"

"Yes. Why?"

"You know why."

How did he know she'd been out last night? "Yes, I do know. The question is, how do you?"

"I'm a light sleeper."

No way they'd woken him. She and Max could walk right up to his house and he'd never know it.

"I don't make noise."

"No. You don't. Which is a little freaky, by the way. But my bedroom window faces the cabin. When lights come on in the middle of the night... I know two plus two equals trouble."

She took another sip. "Only when I'm around."

"Trouble darkened our world before you arrived, Heidi. You're the one bringing the light. Don't ever forget that."

His phone rang and they both groaned.

"Bridget." They said the name at the same time and with the same level of exasperation. That woman never missed an opportunity to interrupt them whenever they were alone together.

"Thank you for the tea," Heidi said as Blake turned back to his office.

"Thank you," he said, "for last night, and the night before, and a week ago."

Wow. He had been paying attention. He also left the door between their offices open, making it easy for her to hear him.

She could picture him as he entered his office, returned to his seat and answered Bridget's call with thinly veiled annoyance. He chuckled as he replaced the phone. Then he drew in a long breath and blew it back out before his fingers flew over his keyboard.

She leaned back in her chair.

Friends made friends tea. Right? Not that Max had ever bothered to learn, but he had no problem with day-old coffee. He couldn't be counted on to appreciate the art form.

After Heidi had invited all the Harrison ladies over for tea one Saturday, Maggie had become enthralled with the whole process. They'd had tea every Saturday since. She'd assumed Blake's insistence on learning to brew a "proper cup of tea," which he always said with a dreadful fake British accent, had been for Maggie's benefit.

Maybe she'd been wrong about his motivation.

Blake poked his head into her office. "Sorry to bother you, but Maggie would like to know if you'll be attending her basketball game Saturday."

Maggie wanted to know, did she?

"It's up to you."

Blake shrugged. "I hate to ask you to give up your Saturday morning, but I can't deny it makes me feel better, safer, when you're there."

Better? Or safer?

"It's not a problem. I'll be there."

"Great. I'll pick you up at nine-thirty so we can ride over together." He gave her a quick smile before leaving the office.

Going to Maggie's games, having the Harrison ladies over for tea, all fit into the framework of her mission. She was able to provide security, and she was learning a lot about the personal side of the business and the family thrust into this drama through no fault of their own.

These people had become friends. Good friends. She would miss them when the case ended, but she'd be forever thankful she'd had the opportunity to spend this time with them.

Max's insinuation about her feelings for Blake squirmed through her brain but she forced them away. She was still in control.

Wasn't she?

Blake Harrison tapped on Heidi's door at 9:30 a.m. on Saturday morning. Funny how he no longer thought of it as the cabin, but as Heidi's house. She answered wearing jeans tucked into boots, a long sweater and the often-present scarf.

As they walked to his car, he had to ask. "What's with the scarves?"

"What?"

"The scarves? You wear one almost every day. You take it off when you're around moving equipment, but then you put it right back on."

"What's your problem with scarves?" She laughed as she slid into the front seat of his car and he closed the door after her. By the time he got behind the wheel, she and Maggie were planning the menu for this afternoon's tea and the issue of scarves was dropped.

Until an hour later as they watched Maggie play her heart out.

"You never answered my question," Heidi said.

"What question?"

"What's your problem with scarves?"

She jumped to her feet and let out a piercing whistle when Maggie scored. She was really good for a five-year-old. Of course, it helped that the goal wasn't much taller than she was.

As Heidi sat back down, Blake nudged her with his elbow. "I never said I had a problem with them. I asked you why you wear them all the time."

She had a mischievous gleam in her eye when she answered. "I'll show you later." She fiddled with the scarf as she turned her attention back to the game. "You won't like it."

Heidi excused herself several times during the game. She'd told his mom and Caroline that crowds made her uncomfortable and she got claustrophobic sitting squished with everyone. At first, he'd assumed she'd made that up to give her an excuse to walk around and scan the area for anything suspicious.

But he'd begun to see how often she spoke the truth, even as she twisted it to suit her purposes. Like with the claustrophobia. That might be a bit of a stretch, but she had told him when they'd first met about how much she hated crowds. She wasn't lying to them, but she was leaving out the part about wanting to make sure there wasn't a madman lurking in the hall waiting to blow the place up.

Same with her knitting. She'd told him it made it easier for her to sit in a crowd if she had a few sharp objects in her hands. Her mom and sister, and even Maggie, thought nothing more of it than that she loved to knit. She pulled her knitting out in all sorts of random places, and did it often enough that no one gave it a second thought. Which was the whole idea.

He enjoyed being able to see beneath the facade to the real person underneath. He'd pushed her too far the night of the Christmas party and she'd slammed the door in his face. He should have left it closed. He'd planned to.

Then she'd taken off to keep tabs on the Kovacs over the holidays. Every day he'd paused at the door to her office, every night he'd check for lights in the cabin. By the time she'd returned at the first of the year, he'd given up on the notion that he would stay out of her way and let her do her job. Something about her kept him coming back for more.

The real Heidi fascinated him and he'd found it impossible not to keep digging.

He prayed he wouldn't live to regret it.

Three hours later, he knocked on her door. The scent of blueberry scones wafted through the screen. His favorite. While he had never been invited to tea—*It's for the ladies, Daddy*, Maggie had informed him—he enjoyed sampling the menu.

"Come on in, it's open."

He followed the sound of her voice into the kitchen. "Smells amazing."

She grinned. "Where's Maggie?"

"She's been at Caroline's this afternoon working on something I'm not allowed to see." He didn't know why he didn't mention he had a birthday coming up. "I'm just here for the food."

"Ah." Heidi nodded.

"You know what they're up to, don't you?"

"I don't know what you're talking about."

"Liar."

She shrugged. "That's why they pay me the big bucks." She stepped behind him and he heard the refrigerator door open. The next thing he knew, he hit the floor. Her scarf was wrapped around his throat. Not tight, but tight enough.

His body reacted before his brain caught up. He kicked his leg out and swept her feet out from under her. She released the scarf as she landed on her rear.

She was back on her feet in seconds, her eyes wide with shock. "You knocked me down!"

"I'm sorry." He couldn't believe he'd done that.

"That'll teach me to forget about that black belt. You've got skills." She laughed as she unwound the scarf from his neck. "Sorry I caught you off guard, but that's kind of the idea."

She offered him a hand to pull him up, but then stepped back. "Are you angry?"

"Of course I'm angry." He could see the confusion, and even some hurt as it spread across her features.

"You did ask why I always wear them, so I figured I'd give a demonstration. I thought you would think it was funny. I'm sorry."

"Why are you apologizing to me?"

"I attacked you with a scarf and you're angry about it. Shouldn't I apologize?"

"I'm not angry at you."

"Well, you shouldn't be upset about me taking you down. It's my job to be able to. I've spent a lot of time training for it and—"

"I don't care about that," Blake said. Maybe he did, a little. "I can't believe I kicked you. I don't go around kicking women."

"You didn't kick me. You executed an impressive sweep. Which I wasn't expecting and landed me on my rear. I'm fine, Blake. No harm, no foul."

"I could have hurt you."

She studied him, her green eyes almost disappearing beneath her furrowed brow, then she sat down on the floor in front of him. "Let's get one thing clear. You were not trying to hurt me. You were defending yourself. And you did it well. If you weren't upset, I would say we need to do this more often."

Was she out of her mind?

"We've been dealing with the drama of the unknown for almost three months. At this stage in an operation, it's hard to stay focused, to stay on guard, especially since there haven't been any attacks lately. It's more important than ever that we stay sharp. We have to be ready for whatever comes at us."

The knock on the door drove both of them to their feet.

He couldn't stop his arms from reaching for her. He put both hands on her upper arms and looked deep into her eyes. She didn't back away, or fight him, but he could see the desire to do both, and maybe even the desire to do something else. "Are you sure you're okay?"

She smiled. "Yes. Are you?"

Good question. The door opened and Maggie's voice broke through the tension. "Are you in there, Miss Heidi?" He needed to talk to Maggie about bursting into other people's houses uninvited.

Heidi turned to the stove and called out, "In here."

Blake left a few minutes later carrying a paper plate full of ham sandwiches and scones. He placed them on the porch swing while he went inside to pour a glass of iced tea. When he came back out, he could hear laughter and conversation bubbling from Heidi's porch.

He finished off the ham sandwiches in three bites and then dove in to the scones. He opened the upcoming week's production schedule from his iPad and scanned through the runs. The last run of the sample batch they were making for the baseball parks would run through Wednesday, a smaller order for the Flight to Win the Fight races would run on Thursday and Friday, along with a handful of specialty batches.

It should be a calm week, but Heidi's words kept niggling at him. It had been two months since someone had tried to kill him. As far as anyone could tell, his dad's stroke had been the fault of heredity, not human manipulation. Heidi spent hours each week doing a stellar job as a quality engineer, and then even more hours trying to determine what Mark was planning.

Sometimes he forgot why she was here, but then there were days when he could feel tension rolling off her in waves. Something had to give, and soon. He didn't know how much longer any of them could stand under the pressure.

TWELVE

Heidi started her third month of work at HPI with a migraine and a bad attitude. Why couldn't it be easy? There were fifty agents working on this case and the only success they'd had was that they'd been able to make some useful recommendations to improve the process at HPI.

And they'd kept Blake Harrison alive. Three months ago, she couldn't have guessed how important that would be to her.

She sat in the observation room and watched the lines running. The smell of blown plastic permeated everything, the sounds all fit with a normal production run and nothing looked out of the ordinary. Another typical Monday.

Markos stepped onto the plant floor. He'd been in the warehouse? Again? She'd noticed him disappearing and reappearing from there more than once, but when she'd followed his route, she'd found nothing but boxes of containers stacked high on pallets, waiting for shipment. Did he go back there to smoke? HPI had a strict no-smoking policy, but TacOps had learned Markos had a serious habit.

Blake appeared at one end of the production line. He was predictable with this routine. Before he left, he walked the lines, spoke to the shift supervisors and then made a pass through the warehouse. As long as everything was running smoothly, he headed home.

She checked her watch. Four-fifteen. Time for her to pack up. Maggie had a bake sale this weekend and she'd promised to teach her how to make scones.

Funny how the Harrison family had accepted her into their world. Caroline treated her like a lifelong friend. Maggie assumed she would be at all games, church services and family outings.

Eleanor Harrison had been too busy with Jeffrey's care to pay her much mind at first. Now that Jeffrey's recovery had reached a point where he didn't require as much assistance, she'd been paying closer attention to Heidi.

And Eleanor Harrison had matchmaking on her mind.

While it was flattering, Heidi wished she could explain how wrong she was for Eleanor's son. Blake Harrison had turned into a good friend, but that was all it could ever be. Sure, he had it all—intelligence, good looks and charm oozing from every pore. He had a wicked sense of humor but tempered it with a compassionate streak that had caught her off guard and touched parts of her she kept locked down.

If they'd met under different circumstances, maybe there could have been something between them. Maybe. She still hadn't decided if his annoying side outweighed his considerate side. But it didn't matter. She had a criminal to catch and even after she took Markos down, the Kovac family would still be out there.

Until she took them out of the game—permanently— Heidi couldn't afford to get too close to anyone.

Blake Harrison had a lovely life, a great family, a wonderful business. When he decided he wanted to add a loving wife to the picture, it wouldn't be her. It couldn't be.

She watched him leave the plant floor and walk into the warehouse. She scanned the area again. Markos was talking to one of the line operators. This was as good a time as any for her to slip out of her hiding spot.

She picked up her iPad and made her way down the

stairs. As she reached the door, a rumble reverberated through the walls. The warehouse. She ran toward the sound.

As she burst through the door, others ran in from different parts of the plant.

"Over here!"

"Quick!"

"Get a forklift!"

The voices rang out from the back of the building and she raced in their direction.

She came around a corner and skidded to a stop. Splintered wood and broken boxes littered the floor. As far as she could tell, an entire shelving unit had collapsed. It must have held both empty pallets and boxes of finished containers because they lay everywhere.

Markos jumped onto a forklift and moved the pallets and boxes he could reach. He didn't look like a man who'd tried to kill someone.

But Heidi knew he had.

Somehow, he'd tampered with those shelves and figured out a way to make them fall when he wanted them to.

She paused long enough to concentrate on what she was seeing, committing the scene to memory. She'd spend time processing it later, but for now, only one question mattered.

Where was Blake?

She waded into the melee and stopped one of the warehouse employees. "Have you seen Blake?"

"Hasn't he already left for the day?"

Maybe he had. Maybe he'd skipped the warehouse and gone on home. Heidi grabbed her phone and dialed Blake's number.

The pile rang.

Everyone froze.

"Blake's in there!"

"What?"

"Blake?"

The voices took on a new urgency. Everyone worked to pull the boxes and pallets out of the pile.

As they neared the floor, Heidi eased her way closer.

Father, please.

"Over here!"

One of the second-shift line supervisors held up Blake's iPad. Why wasn't he saying anything?

"Blake!" Heidi yelled and others joined in. "Shh," she said and everyone went quiet, listening for any sound. Nothing. They continued moving pallets and boxes.

"There!" She ran to him while some of the men pulled the last remaining boxes away.

Blake lay on his side, blood pooling on the floor. *No. No! Not him!*

Someone screamed.

Another voice called out, "I'm calling 9-1-1."

Heidi made eye contact with the employees standing nearby. "Keep moving this mess away. We're going to need a clear path to get a stretcher to him."

She stepped over a shattered pallet and knelt beside him.

"Come on, Blake. Don't do this to me." She couldn't let herself think about a world where his smile didn't start her day.

She leaned closer. Breath. Yes!

"He's breathing!" A cheer went up. "ETA on the ambulance?"

"They're on the way."

"Tell them to hurry!"

Heidi tried to get a fix on where the blood was coming from. Would moving him cause more harm? She couldn't bear to be responsible for a spinal injury, but nothing could be worse than if he bled to death while she watched.

She eased herself to the floor behind him and stretched

a tentative hand toward him. She touched his head with the lightest pressure she could manage. His hair was sticky with blood, but there were no other obvious injuries.

The whine of sirens reached her ears. Blake hadn't opened his eyes or responded to any of the chaos around him. Maybe that was for the best.

The EMTs arrived and Heidi had to work not to react. Richards? She knew some of the TacOps team had combat trauma experience and they knew their stuff. She had no idea how they'd gotten here, and in an ambulance no less. She'd ask later.

"What happened?" Agent Richards asked her.

"Looks like the shelving unit collapsed."

"Has he been moved at all?"

"No."

Heidi stood back as they put a neck brace on Blake. With a gentleness that didn't match their heft, they strapped him to a backboard, loaded him onto a gurney and rolled him to the waiting ambulance.

She got in with them.

"Ma'am, you'll need to drive your own car." She couldn't tell if Agent Richards was trying to be a jerk or trying to maintain his cover. It didn't matter.

"I am not getting out of this ambulance, and if you don't get him to the hospital promptly you'll be facing litigation." Not to mention the butt-kicking she'd personally administer.

Richards nodded at one of the other agents and the doors closed. As soon as they drove away, he hit her on the shoulder.

"You should have stayed behind."

"I don't think so."

"What if this was intentional? What if Markos uses the confusion to hide the evidence? Did you think about that?"

She hadn't. Heaven help her. All she'd thought about was the man lying on the gurney who still hadn't opened his eyes.

Richards was right.

How could she have been so stupid?

He didn't say anything else as he checked vitals and pupils and tried to stop the bleeding. They rode in silence for a full five minutes until he asked her to hand him a stack of gauze pads from the shelf behind her.

When he took them, he winked. "I had a feeling you might not be bringing your A game, so I left a few men behind."

Heidi pinched the bridge of her nose. "Thank you."

What more could she say? What did it indicate about her if everyone on this case knew her feelings could compromise the investigation at any time? What did it mean that she had these feelings in the first place?

She bounced along in the back of the ambulance and tried to rationalize her reasons for going with them. She had good ones.

Didn't she?

Blake had been harmed and someone would need to provide security for him at the hospital. She couldn't let them take him there alone in this condition.

Of course, it would have only taken one phone call to have a team of agents waiting for them, ready to stay close.

Why had she been compelled to be with him?

This case was messing with her.

So was this man.

The first thing that filtered into Blake's consciousness was the smell. A smell that was all too familiar.

How had he wound up in a hospital again? He tried to open his eyes, but they didn't want to cooperate.

"Hey."

That was a voice worth waking up for. He tried again. Nope.

A hand squeezed his. "Don't fight it. You're going to be fine. Although this time you do have a concussion."

He squeezed Heidi's hand and tried to remember how he'd gotten here. He'd checked on the line. Everything had appeared to be running smoothly and the first batch of the run had been first-quality all the way through. No reason to suspect they wouldn't end the evening on a high note.

He'd made a pass through the warehouse. Hadn't he? He couldn't remember anything past checking on the line. Heidi would know.

He didn't bother trying to make his eyes open. He focused on finding his lips. "Wha—" He tried to swallow.

"Here." Something cold touched his lips. Ice? He opened his mouth and a cool chip slid down his throat. Much better. "What happened?"

"You don't remember?"

He shook his head and regretted it. Pain shot through his skull. The upside was he got his eyes open. Heidi's face perched inches from his own.

"Moving might not be a good idea."

"Ya think?"

She chuckled. "Glad to see you're as annoying as ever."

"Only with you."

"Ha."

"You still haven't told me what happened."

"I'm trying to give you time to remember."

Oh. "Can you tell me where I am?"

"Where do you think you are?"

"I know I'm in the hospital. Am I in ICU or some sort of trauma unit?"

"Nope. Still in the ER."

That meant he hadn't been out of it for too long. He tried to think. "Did I ride in an ambulance?"

"Yes."

"Were you fighting with someone? No. Wait. Someone was fussing at you. I remember wanting to tell them to leave you alone."

Heidi didn't say anything. She didn't have to. Bits and pieces of the ride were coming back to him. He still couldn't remember how he'd wound up in the ambulance, but he'd heard someone tell her she should have stayed behind. And something about her feelings?

No. He must have been dreaming. The agent must have been teasing her. And what did it matter? She'd never see him as more than a good friend. She'd made that clear. Which was good, because even if he did have feelings for her, which he didn't, he could never allow himself to act on those feelings.

He had Maggie to think about. Maggie needed stability and there was nothing stable about Heidi Zimmerman. She spent half her life undercover in dangerous settings. A woman like Heidi could disappear for weeks, months, maybe even years.

As much as he hated to think about it, Heidi's job put her in jeopardy every single day. Could he risk a relationship with a woman with a life as dangerous as Heidi's?

If it were just him? Maybe.

But when he added Maggie into the picture?

No.

Besides, even if Heidi did care for him in some small way, she'd made it clear that her mission in life was to bring down the Kovacs. It would be hard to do that from North Carolina and he couldn't pick up the entire HPI operation and move it to Virginia.

No. Nothing about this would ever work. It couldn't.

"Anything else coming back to you?" He heard the fear

in her question. She probably didn't want him to know the agents were teasing her about her feelings for him.

"A lot of jostling. Maybe some people yelling?" He pushed his brain to the edges of his memory. "Was I in the warehouse?"

"Yes," she said and he heard the relief. "An entire section of shelves collapsed. We found you buried under pallets and boxes."

"We?"

"It made a lot of noise. I think everyone not running a line came to dig you out."

"How did you know to look for me?"

"I tried your phone."

"Good idea."

"Thanks. I've been known to have one from time to time."

He tried to remember the sequence of events, but nothing about what she said rang a bell. "Did Mark do it?"

"We'll know more after the team your dad has hired to inspect all the shelves gets back to us."

"He hired a team?"

"I may have recommended them. They'll be able to determine what caused those shelves to fall and if there was a trigger. There's a problem with the Markos theory, though. I was watching the line from the observation room and he wasn't in the warehouse when it happened. Either he had help, or he had a way to trigger it remotely, or it was a total fluke."

"I'm not prepared to buy into the fluke theory."

"Me, neither."

"What's my status?"

"No broken bones, although I have no idea how that's even possible. The nasty cut on your head needed twenty stitches. You should be glad you don't remember that part. The head wound explains the amount of blood we saw. Unless you're having trouble moving your limbs, it looks like your biggest complaint is going to be a massive headache. And you can't drive for the next five days."

Great.

She hesitated. "In order to facilitate the inspection of the warehouse, your dad has decided to shut down the plant until Thursday. He's going to pay everyone for the missed time."

"Your idea?"

"Maybe."

"I don't like that one."

"I didn't expect you would."

She was right, though. Shutting down the plant for several days would give whatever this team was a chance to go over the whole place with a microscope. They'd be looking for anything and everything, and it could protect their employees and his family from further harm. "It might give Mark time to plan something worse."

"I don't think time is his problem."

"What is?"

"You."

"Why me?"

"I have no idea."

THIRTEEN

Blake refused to stay away from the office on Wednesday. He wanted to be there. If they found anything, he wanted to see it.

Heidi had not approved of his plan. "Why don't you take it easy? I'll let you know if anything happens."

He appreciated her concern, but he was sick of taking it easy…even though his head still throbbed, and he wasn't supposed to drive for three more days. Stupid concussion. He had work to do. This unplanned shutdown would put them behind, but they could make up for the lost time. Assuming they kept the quality in check.

He walked through the production area. Agents roamed about with flashlights or Geiger counters or devices he didn't recognize.

He walked through the warehouse and spotted Heidi near the collapsed shelving units. She was talking to an agent and even though he couldn't hear the conversation, he could tell she wasn't happy. She had one hand on her hip, the other she ran through her hair the way she did when something bothered her.

She smiled when she saw him, and that smile made his insides squirm. She'd been distant since he'd come home from the hospital and, to be fair, so had he. He couldn't forget what he'd heard in the ambulance. The idea that she might have some sort of feelings for him beyond friendship presented itself every time she came into view.

He could not fall for her. *Why her, Father? Why now?*

Hadn't he been through enough? He'd loved Lana, and while their marriage hadn't been perfect, he'd made every effort to make it work. Even after she'd admitted to the addiction and the embezzlement, he'd been willing to try, but she'd made it clear her feelings for him had never been more than a passing fancy that had long since shriveled into outright disdain.

He'd been sure he'd never find anyone else he'd be willing to take a chance on, and with the way he lived his life, the likelihood of meeting someone had been slim.

Then Heidi had dropped into his world with her crazy hair, her badge and that gun she kept tucked in her waistband, all contrasting with the woman he'd discovered her to be. A woman who loved tea and scones and dainty sandwiches, who could play Candy Land with Maggie for hours and had even taught her how to knit a dishcloth.

A woman who was worth risking his heart. Maybe even worth the risk to Maggie. Maggie had strong women in her life, but what would it be like for her to have Heidi as a stepmother?

What was he thinking? Even if he could get past the danger of her job, there was one other pesky problem. She hadn't moved here. She had a home in Virginia and a desk in a building owned by the FBI. When this case ended, she'd go back to the life she'd been living.

He didn't want to think about how he would go back to the life he'd been living.

It would never be the same.

"Blake, I'd like you to meet Kyle Richards. You may not remember, but Kyle was one of the EMTs who took you to the hospital. He's also the lead agent on the TacOps team assigned to this case."

Kyle extended his hand. "Good to see you up and around. I imagine you're still feeling that crack to the noggin, though."

They shook hands. "Thanks for getting me to the hospital in one piece. I appreciate it."

"Just doing my job." He pointed to the mess of metal behind him. "I was telling Z as far as we can tell, these shelves weren't screwed together right."

"How do you mean?"

Agent Richards picked up a metal support piece. "See this here?" He pointed to a bolt hole. "At least half of these pieces had bolts in them at one time, but they aren't here now." He pointed to the pile. "We've been through it piece by piece. The only explanation we can come up with is someone has been removing the bolts. Maybe all at once. Maybe a few at a time. Either way, this setup was going to come down sooner or later."

He tossed the piece back into the pile. "What we haven't found is any sort of trigger. Either someone helped it fall as you came by, or it was a total fluke."

Heidi met Blake's gaze. "I don't believe in flukes," he said and caught the twinkle in her eye.

"Me, neither," Richards said.

"Who brought it down?" Heidi asked the question, but she clearly didn't expect an answer.

Richards rubbed his chin. "Somebody who knows how to cover their tracks."

Heidi and Richards exchanged a look that spoke volumes. They were worried. And if they were worried, he should be petrified.

On Saturday morning, Blake rolled over and grabbed his phone. Five o'clock. He threw back the covers and went straight to the coffeepot.

What a week. They'd had the plant shut down until

Thursday. Then his dad's cousin had passed away in Vermont and his parents had flown out yesterday for the funeral. Caroline had gone to a spa somewhere in Georgia for a long-planned weekend with her college roommates.

His former in-laws, the Petersons, had taken Maggie home from her ball game last night and he and Heidi had wound up going to dinner.

It hadn't been a date. They were hungry and needed food.

But they'd sat in the Thai restaurant until it closed at ten. Then they'd stood in the driveway and talked until after midnight.

The funny thing was they hadn't talked about the case or the plant. They'd talked about other stuff. Pet peeves, favorite foods, books, movies, even places they'd love to visit. They talked about college and his grandparents and her godparents. Safe topics for the most part, although every now and then he got the impression that she was holding back.

The difference from this conversation and the one they'd had at Christmas was that he didn't think she was holding back because she didn't trust him, but because she was trying to protect him. From what horror, he had no idea.

When they said their reluctant good-nights, it was with the promise to meet in the driveway at 9:00 a.m. to get some breakfast.

He couldn't get a handle on it, but something had changed last night. The air had been thick with words unspoken and questions unanswered.

He had no idea what was happening but he needed to get his head on straight before he saw her again. If he got moving, he'd have plenty of time to head to his favorite spot and spend time in prayer.

He and the Lord needed to talk. He couldn't understand why God would drop a woman like Heidi into his life only to snatch her back out of it. It seemed cruel. But what if it wasn't? What if a way to make it work existed but he hadn't figured it out yet?

He filled a thermos with coffee, grabbed a couple of granola bars and three fun-size Snickers bars and picked up his cell phone, keys and Bible before he walked out the door. He knew the path well enough to walk it in the dark, but he flicked on the flashlight anyway. No need to take unnecessary risks. Heidi would already never let him hear the end of it if she found out he was hiking with a concussion.

Thirty minutes later, he'd set his Bible, phone and coffee on the large boulder stretched out over the edge of the waterfall that emptied into the river running behind the plant. He loved it here. The peacefulness, the solitude, the calm.

He bowed his head and waited in the predawn silence. This place was sacred to him. A place where God met him. He knew there was nothing unique or special about this boulder, only that this was where he got quiet and listened.

So he listened and waited for answers to come.

Heidi's phone jarred her to consciousness and she was thankful for the disruption. The nightmare had been coming more often. The same one she'd been having for fifteen years. Sunshine and a cool breeze on her face morphed in an instant to darkness and heat as her clothes melted into her skin and she shrieked in agony. That's when she woke up, face covered in sweat, or maybe tears. She could never be sure.

She hadn't cried over her scarred body and broken dreams in years. At least, not when conscious. But last night, the way Blake had looked at her—

She groaned and wiped her face with the damp sheet.

He had no idea how messed up she was. Or how much damage the long-sleeved shirts covered. She'd gotten away with hiding it to this point. The mountains were cold in the winter, and she'd told everyone she was cold-natured. No one questioned it.

They would in the heat of summer, when tank tops and shorts became the norm. She didn't need or want their pity, but she dreaded the day she saw that look in Blake's eyes. The one she'd seen before from other men when they cringed away from the puckered and pink scars covering half her body.

When it happened, she would never recover.

Her phone squawked again, this time with a text message instead of a call.

WAKE UP AND CALL ME

Agent Richards? Why would he be calling her at five-thirty in the morning?

She pulled on a pair of jeans as she dialed.

"It's about time you called."

"Your text—"

"No time. Do you have any idea why Blake Harrison is hiking in the woods behind the plant?"

Heidi rubbed a hand over her face. "What?"

"Blake Harrison is walking around in the woods behind the plant."

"Now?"

"Until two minutes ago. The locater we have on his phone stopped moving. Looks like it's beside a river."

"He knows these woods. I guess he went out for an early-morning hike. What's the problem?" She slipped a sweatshirt over her head.

"The problem is the other GPS locator in the area."

She didn't need to ask, but she had to. "Who?"

"Kovac. He's almost to the same spot."

"No!" Heidi threw the phone onto the bed as she raced

to pull on tennis shoes. She grabbed two handguns and strapped them to her waist. If someone saw her, tough.

She picked up the phone and ran down the stairs. "I'm headed out there. Call in the cavalry."

"Z. You need to wait for backup."

"I don't have time. If Kovac acts fast, I need to be able to stop him. Send his location to my phone and get the team moving in this direction."

She heard him giving orders as she pulled a rifle from behind the refrigerator and slid the strap over her shoulder and back.

"We'll blow your cover."

"Do you think I care?"

Heidi ran out the screen door and hit the hiking trail at a steady run, thankful she had a good idea of where she was headed.

"No, ma'am. I have everyone converging on his location. Keep your phone on so I'll have some ears."

"Fine." She slid the phone into her jacket pocket and ran faster.

There was no good reason for Kovac to be following Blake up this mountain. The Harrisons had several picnic shelters and hiking paths laid out for the use of their employees, but the spot where Blake was—the one he had told her about—was nowhere near those public access areas.

How could Kovac have known he'd be there at this time of day? Was he tracking Blake? And if he was, why hadn't they caught on to it? How had they missed it?

She'd been a fool. Distracted. Incompetent. Letting stupid emotions keep her from focusing on the issue at hand. Her idiocy may have already gotten Blake killed.

She pulled her phone back to her ear. "Richards?"

"Yes, ma'am."

"Do you still have Blake's phone active?"

"Yes, ma'am. Why?"

"If it disappears, you let me know."

Richards didn't say anything for a moment. "You're going to get to him in time."

"Are you a praying man, Richards?"

"At times like this."

"Good. Pray hard. That's an order."

"Yes, ma'am."

She put the phone back in her pocket and pushed on. She could run at this pace for several miles before she had to slow down, but the bumpy uphill terrain added a degree of difficulty. Spraining her ankle could be a death sentence for Blake.

She'd hiked up here once when she'd been familiarizing herself with the Harrison property. She ran until she thought she was close and then slowed and slid the rifle over her head.

"Richards?"

"Kovac is three hundred yards to the north of your current location. He hasn't moved in the past ten minutes. Blake is three hundred yards northeast. I'm guessing Kovac is watching and waiting for an opportunity."

She took a few deep breaths. "I'm going to get in closer. Where's my backup?"

"Ten guys are headed up the trail behind you, but they don't know the path the way you must have. They're moving at a good clip, but…"

"Have them pull up when they get to this location and come in slow."

"Yes, ma'am. Good luck, Z. I'm praying."

Heidi checked her weapons and eased forward through a natural curve in the trail.

There. She could hear the waterfall churning in the distance and she could imagine where Blake sat.

Markos Kovac leaned against a tree, hands on his knees.

She could see his chest heaving. He'd hotfooted it up here, but he'd left himself too winded to finish the job.

Thank You, Father.

She moved closer and knelt behind a spruce to watch him through the scope. As far as she could tell, he had a gun and a…baseball bat? Surely he didn't intend to club—

Oh.

Yes, that would make sense. This murder would look like a tragic accident. If he could sneak up behind Blake and hit him with the bat, even if he didn't kill him with the blow, he could knock him out and shove him over the edge. There would be a good chance the impact at the bottom would disguise the trauma. Everyone would think Blake had slipped.

Of course, he'd brought the gun as backup. He had every intention of killing Blake this morning, she had no doubt. If the accidental plunge to his death didn't work, he'd shoot him and toss the gun in the river.

And it wasn't a bad plan. Or it wouldn't have been if the TacOps team hadn't been watching.

She'd owe those guys for eternity.

She weighed her options. She could try to shoot Markos from here, but a branch could deflect the bullet. She could scoot closer and hope the roar of the water would drown out her approach. She could call Blake on his cell and tell him to get out of there, but if he moved, she couldn't predict Kovac's response. He might shoot him on the spot before she could do anything.

Father, help me.

She picked her way through the trees, thankful the ground was moist from recent snow and the leaves blanketing the forest floor bent instead of crackling as she stepped on them.

She'd gotten within fifty yards when Markos moved toward Blake. Slow and deliberate. She followed behind him at a faster pace, relying on the sound of his own movement to disguise hers.

Her mind raced for a way to get them all off this mountain alive, but no matter which scenario she considered, someone wound up dead every time. Kovac wouldn't surrender, but maybe she could disarm him. She'd seen one gun. And the bat. But she had no way of knowing what sort of arsenal he hid under the field jacket he wore.

She wanted to take him alive. He was the key to unlocking the door to his family's plans for HPI.

She slid through the brush behind him, shrinking the distance between them. At this point, if he turned, she'd be exposed, but that didn't matter anymore. She slid the rifle back over her neck and pulled her Glock out of the holster. At this range, she could drop him if she had to.

He paused twenty feet from Blake's position. If he would sit tight for five more minutes, she'd have a team of agents at her disposal and they'd be able to wrap this up in a nice neat bow.

Kovac moved.

So much for waiting on backup.

FOURTEEN

Blake finished his coffee. He still didn't have any answers, but the peace he'd been missing for weeks had settled over him. He knew deep in his soul God had not dropped the ball. He needed to wait. And trust.

"Don't do it, Markos!" Heidi's voice rang out from behind him.

He turned and for one long second, everything froze. The man he knew as Mark Hammond stood three feet away. A large gun protruded from his waistband, but the immediate threat came from the baseball bat Mark gripped with both hands.

Ten feet from Mark, Heidi stood exposed, weapon drawn.

Mark turned toward Heidi.

Before Blake could blink, Mark drew his gun.

Heidi and Mark fired at the same time.

Heidi ran in a crouch toward them. "Blake! Run!"

Blake looked back to Mark. He lay on the ground, blood seeping through his jacket, but he managed to lift his arm and take aim. Blake kicked Mark's arm and his gun flew into the woods.

Heidi stood two feet away, chest heaving, hair flying around her face, eyes burning as she glared at Mark, her gun pointed at his chest.

"Markos Kovac, you are under arrest for attempted murder."

Mark looked at Heidi, then at Blake. "I am truly sorry."
He reached for his belt. Did he have another gun?

"Blake! *Run!*" This time, Heidi grabbed Blake's arm and
pulled him as she dashed away from Mark.

What was going on? She had a gun on him. What did
she think—

The ground rocked beneath him and an explosive force
knocked him off his feet and away from Heidi. Burning
branches rained down on them and as the dust cleared,
Blake looked back toward Mark.

Mark was gone.

His gun lay a few feet away, and Blake scrambled for
it. Where had Mark—?

As he reached for the gun, his brain made sense of the
scene and the awful truth registered.

Severed body parts lay strewn over the burning mountain. A stench he couldn't describe, but would never forget, filled the air.

"Heidi?"

She had known. Somehow she'd known what Mark intended and she'd pulled him to safety.

"Heidi?"

Oh, no. "No!"

Heidi's jacket glowed with fire. She yanked the rifle over
her head, dropped to the ground and rolled.

He rushed to her side and grabbed one sleeve to help her
pull her arm out. Her eyes were wide and the terror in them
frightened him more than anything he'd witnessed yet.

Free of the jacket, she yanked her smoking sweatshirt
over her head and threw it to the ground. She stood and
stomped on both the jacket and the sweatshirt, over and over
before she collapsed to her knees, sobs shaking her body.

She was in just a tank top now, and on her exposed skin
he could see the patchwork of scars from her neck down
the back of her arms. The skin stretched and puckered in

odd places, and had a pinkish tint that didn't match the rest of her olive-toned complexion. The scarring could be seen on her chest above the edges of her shirt. He could only assume it covered most of her torso.

What had happened to her?

Blake knelt beside her. "It's okay, honey. It's okay. It's over." He pulled her into his arms and held her as she shook. Was she in shock? Having a panic attack? He couldn't make sense of her reaction. She was the bravest woman he'd ever known and not the type to fall apart over an explos—

He rested his cheek on the top of her head as the pieces fell into place. The scars. Burns. Horrible burns. She'd told him the Kovacs had scarred her for life. He'd assumed it was a metaphorical statement, but now he realized she'd been telling him the literal truth.

"Baby, I'm sorry. The fire is out, honey." He kept up a steady stream of encouragement as her shaking slowed to trembling. She relaxed out of the tight ball she'd curled into and leaned her head against his chest as her breathing eased.

"They killed them."

She took a deep shuddering breath, and he hastened to reassure her.

"You don't have to tell—"

"I was sixteen. They placed me in a foster family that had a twenty-one-year-old son…"

A violent tremor rocked through her. Blake fought back the nausea as the implications of what she was saying registered. "You don't have to—"

"Yes, I do!" Her voice shook as she yelled at him. "I do! Because you have to understand."

He had no idea what to do. He sensed that she expected him to push her away, so he held her. Tight. She squirmed in his arms. He refused to let go. She could break free if she wanted to, and if she put up a serious objection, he'd release her immediately.

For a moment, he thought she might punch him.

Then the air whooshed out of her and she went limp in his arms.

"When he came after me, I ran. Rachel was twenty, working at the restaurant I stopped in to get warm. She asked a few questions that I thought I'd deflected, but fifteen minutes later, this couple shows up and slides into my booth. Her parents, David and Angie Thompson.

"I still don't know why I told them everything, but I did. Next thing I knew, I was in a clean house with a clean room just for me, wearing clean clothes. I fell off the grid and they caught me. Put me in school. Became my family."

She sniffed.

"It was the happiest year of my life. I made good grades, went to church, discovered there was Someone who had loved me forever and would love me forever. Fell head over heels in love with Jesus and truly believed my life would be glorious and wonderful forever."

She shrugged in his arms. "I didn't know anything about Rachel's boyfriend for a while. Even after I met him, I didn't know who he was—who his family was. I didn't know how much danger we were all in."

More pieces of the puzzle fell into place. "Was he a Kovac?"

"Yes. Jozsef Kovac. He went by Joe. Markos's oldest brother. He was the apple of his grandfather's eye, which was the only reason he hadn't yet faced any consequences for his refusal to join the family business. But his uncles wouldn't stop pressuring him. When he and Rachel told the Thompsons what was going on, they were horrified. Not that she'd fallen in love with the grandson of a crime boss, but that they intended to elope and disappear to avoid his family's retaliation."

She swallowed hard.

"They should have stuck to that plan. It would have saved their lives."

"The Kovacs found out?"

"Oh, yeah. Mr. Thompson had a lot of connections, and he'd agreed to help them. The plan was to set them up in Canada. In Vancouver. Things were almost finalized, and as far as anyone knew, no one in the Kovac family had a clue."

"How did they find out?"

"I still don't know for sure. I suspect they were being followed. They may have even bugged them. Either way, someone in the Kovac family decided to make an example of them. I believe it was one of his uncles. His grandfather is a horrible, violent man, but he loved him, and so did his father. But some of his uncles are worse than his grandfather ever thought about being, and one of them gave the order.

"We were at home. All of us. The Thompsons, Rachel, Joe and me. It was going to be our last meal together before they ran. Mrs. Thompson asked me to go out to the garage to get some Cokes out of the fridge. I remember I had my hands full of cans. Then everything exploded."

He squeezed her tighter and rocked back and forth as he would when comforting Maggie.

"I don't remember much after that. Heat and pain. My clothes melted into my back. It took weeks of skin grafts and surgeries and—"

What could he say? He held her and prayed.

"Uncle Frank was Rachel's godfather, and even before then, he'd decided he was my godfather, too. He and Aunt Ginny had welcomed me into the family because the Thompsons had. Mr. Thompson must have confided in Uncle Frank, because when I regained consciousness, they were there. He'd arranged for it to look like I was killed in the blast. I left the hospital with a new name and a new face and strict orders never to get anywhere near the Kovacs."

"I'm getting the impression that you don't follow orders very well."

She barked a mirthless laugh. "No. Uncle Frank gave up trying to keep me from going after them and insisted if I was going to play with fire, I at least do it right. I spent my summers learning all sorts of law enforcement techniques. Joined the FBI straight out of college and then went into the organized-crime division. Became the agency's expert on the Kovacs.

"And, here I am." She swiped at the tears on her cheeks. "I'm sorry for the meltdown. I don't like fire."

"You can melt down on me anytime."

She tried to pull away. He held her closer. "Where do you think you're going?"

"I have a job to do, Blake." The sadness in her words cut him to the quick. "We've got a pulverized Kovac scattered all over the place. The family will notice his absence and we need to have a plan for how we're going to handle it. I have to call Uncle Frank, and process the scene, and try to find Katarina Kovac before she does a runner."

"You can do all that in a minute. First, I need you to answer one question."

"What?"

"How did you know he was here?"

"The TacOps team got an alert when he closed in on your position. They called me."

"Just you?"

"There's a team on the way up the mountain. They'll be here any second."

As if on cue, the unmistakable sound of people running toward them pierced the morning air.

Max broke through first.

"Kovac?"

"Blew up."

Max's eyes widened in horror as he took in the scene

and then filled with compassion when he saw the smoking remains of Heidi's jacket and sweatshirt. He knelt beside them. "Z? You okay?"

"Yeah."

Max looked at Blake for confirmation. "No," Blake disagreed. "She was on fire."

Max's reaction proved Blake's suspicion that he knew what had happened in Heidi's past. Blake fought back the little green monster.

Max put one hand on Heidi's arm. "Why don't you take a few more minutes while we secure the scene?"

"I'm fine."

"I have no doubt you will be. Sit tight."

He squeezed her arm and then returned to the group of agents standing a few feet away, their expressions ranging from shock to dismay. He gave orders and they dispersed in groups, some back down the trail, others around the explosion site. Heidi had sat still through it all, her head resting on his chest, but when a chopper circled overhead, looking for a place to land, she pulled away.

"Time for me to get back to work." She gave him a wan smile. "Thanks."

He'd kept his hands away from her skin, afraid of how she might react to his touch, but now he risked it and gently ran his hand down her arm.

She flinched. "You don't have to do that."

"Do what?"

"Pretend it doesn't matter."

"What doesn't matter?" Had she hit her head? Could she be that sensitive about her scars?

"I know what I look like."

"Do you?"

"I've been looking at myself every day for fifteen years. Trust me. You think you'll get used to it and it won't matter, but you won't and it will."

He almost asked how she could think so little of him. Then he saw Max watching them and he got the distinct impression that if he didn't tread lightly, Max would make him regret it. She got to her feet, brushed dirt from her legs and tank top and walked over to one of the agents kneeling beside something that looked disturbingly like an arm.

She shivered in the breeze. If he offered her his jacket, would she get the wrong idea? Would she assume he wanted her to cover up her skin so he didn't have to look at it?

Max walked up to him and extended a hand to help him up. When he got to his feet, Max nodded in Heidi's direction. "You have your work cut out for you, bro."

"Do you know why she's so sensitive?"

Max shrugged. "Took some fierce teasing in college from girls who didn't have enough sense to know she could have killed them in their sleep and gotten away with it. Then a boyfriend dumped her over it."

"Was that the real reason or did she assume?"

"Sara says the guy was a real jerk. Took her to a party but asked her to wear long sleeves so she wouldn't gross his friends out."

Blake swallowed back the bile that rose in his throat. What kind of idiot—

"It's stupid, and she knows it. But at the time, she didn't have anyone to help her process it. Sara says it's a combination of post-traumatic stress and survivor's guilt. The only family she ever loved died and as much as Frank and Ginny tried, she was already in her late teens and badly traumatized by the time she came to them. There was only so much they could do to help her. When we met, she still had a lot of anger. Now?" He looked at her and shrugged. "I think she wants it to be over, but she can't walk away."

"It's hard for me to believe a woman as brilliant as Heidi would struggle with a few scars."

"I can't argue with you there, but when it comes to this

stuff, she's still sixteen. She still has nightmares, and she avoids fireplaces and fireworks. I think in some ways, she believes if she could put the Kovacs away, make them pay for what they did, then she'd be able to let it go. Until then…"

Heidi looked in their direction and Blake could tell she knew they'd been talking about her. She rolled her eyes and walked away.

Max snorted. "Like I said…"

"Got any advice?"

"Tell her the truth. Whatever it is."

Heidi stalked around the mountainside. Her ears rang from the detonation and the stench of burned flesh threatened to make her sick. No one ever got used to that smell.

The forensics team would arrive soon, and she needed to call Uncle Frank with an update, but she couldn't do it yet. She needed to get her emotions back on an even keel after that humiliating breakdown in Blake's arms.

He'd been great. Kicking the gun away had saved her life. She needed to thank him but she'd been avoiding eye contact. She needed to grow up and get over herself. Yes, half of her body had been burned to a crisp, but she still lived and she could still fight. She didn't need people to think of her as beautiful or desirable to do what she needed to do.

But waiting for the look in Blake's eyes to change from appreciation, maybe even infatuation, to the inevitable pity, was going to drive her insane.

He came beside her as she knelt by a shoe blown thirty feet from the blast site. "I want to ask you some things, but I'm afraid you'll take them the wrong way."

This should be interesting. "Go ahead."

"I have two questions. First, is your skin more sensitive where it was burned?"

Not the question she'd been expecting. "What do you mean?"

"I'm wondering about nerve endings. Do you feel heat, cold, touch, more or less?"

Oh. "I do get cold easier. I also overheat easier because my skin doesn't sweat the way it should. As for touch, I honestly don't remember."

She remembered his hand running down the side of her arm. The tingling sensation spreading through her whole body at his touch. Maybe the correct answer was she felt more when he was the one touching her?

"Why?"

He shrugged. Poor guy. He looked miserable. And why wouldn't he be? He'd had his morning solitude destroyed by a maniac trying to kill him. And then he'd seen a man blow himself up. Not what he'd had in mind for this day.

"Because I wanted to tell you I thought your skin is very soft, and I also wanted to ask you if you'd like my sweatshirt because I'm afraid you're cold, but I'm worried you'll have this bizarre notion that I want you to cover up. If you want to wear tank tops year-round, you'll get no objection from me. Although it might be hard for me to get any work done because I'll be distracted."

Heidi had no idea what to make of that. It had come out of the blue and left her abnormally speechless. She managed a strangled "What?"

Blake knelt down and forced her to look him in the eyes. "Are you cold?"

She could say no. If anyone else had asked, she'd say no, but she'd run all the way to the waterfall and had been sweating before having to take off her sweatshirt. Not only did the tank top provide minimal coverage to her skin, it was also damp. She'd been avoiding asking anyone for a sweater because she didn't want to be seen as weak. Blake held her gaze, waiting for her to answer. And he'd already proven how good he was at knowing when she was shading the truth.

She sighed. "Yes. I am."

He pulled off his jacket and dropped it to the ground. His T-shirt lifted as he pulled the sweatshirt over his head and gave Heidi a view of an impressive set of abs. "Here," he said. He tugged his T-shirt down and handed her the sweatshirt. "It will swallow you whole, but it should keep you warm."

"You'll be cold now." His sweatshirt was a nice thick fleece. His jacket wasn't much more than a windbreaker.

"I'll be fine." He shrugged into his coat.

She hesitated.

"Do you need some help putting it on?" He grinned.

"No. Thanks." She slid the fleece over her head and relaxed into the warmth. Her body had tensed from the chill in the air and now it wanted to go limp. The scent of him was everywhere. In her hair, wafting into her face every time she moved.

She liked it.

Maybe too much.

She might need to find a different sweater.

Blake stood close. "Better?"

"Much. Thank you."

Blake stuck his hands in his jacket pocket and looked around the scene. "Now what?"

"Things are about to get messy."

"About to?"

Good point. "I have to call Uncle Frank and tell him Kovac blew himself to bits. Which means we have nothing to go on in terms of figuring out what he was after. We will try to take his wife in for questioning, but she'll lawyer up."

"There's nothing you can do to keep her?"

"Unless we find proof of something in the home, or find some way to connect her to his activities…and let's not forget we have no proof of any illegal activity on his part…then we won't be able to charge her. The Kovacs don't do jail time."

She turned and studied the scene. Something flitted through her brain, begging for attention, but she couldn't quite grasp it. She closed her eyes and perched on a fallen log. She'd learned if she took the time to replay an event, clues popped up that her subconscious had recorded, but she hadn't noticed in the moment.

Max asked Blake what was going on.

"I don't know. She's in the middle of a conversation and just drops. Is she okay?"

Max chuckled. "Watch and learn. Knowing Heidi, she'll have solved the case by the time she stands up."

Heidi tuned them out again. Replayed what she'd seen, heard, felt, smelled. She dismissed everything personal, her fear of being too late and her relief when she wasn't, and focused on what she'd seen.

Markos had waited a long time to make his move. He'd been in one spot for at least fifteen minutes. His delay had given her time to arrive and warn Blake.

Markos hadn't shot Blake. It would have been the one sure way to kill him. Making it look like an accident wasn't a bad idea, but if you needed him dead, why not choose the option that would guarantee it?

She focused in on Markos's face. He'd shot at her, but either he was a lousy shot or— "He didn't want to kill me."

"What?" Blake and Max spoke in unison and when Heidi opened her eyes she found them hovering over her.

She held up a hand and closed her eyes again. His face. The delay in killing Blake. After Blake had kicked his gun away, he'd lain there, looking at the two of them, and then he'd said he was sorry. Sorry for what? For all the trouble? For what he'd already done? For trying to kill them?

A mobster who's sorry for his actions? That did not fit the profile unless—

"Z?" Max's worried voice broke her out of her contemplation. "Throw us a bone."

"I don't have it yet."

"Make it snappy. We're dying here."

"Okay, but I'm thinking out loud." She sat on the ground and crossed her legs. Blake and Max joined her.

"We don't know why Kovac came here, but we know there has to be a reason. A criminal reason. He moves south with no one but his wife, and gets a job? No way a Kovac would do that without an ulterior motive. We've got no idea what his plan is, but we know whatever it is, he—or maybe the senior Kovacs—decided the Harrisons were a liability. So they start trying to pick them off."

"I'd agree with all of that," Max said.

"But I think we have to acknowledge the attempts on Blake's life have been pretty pitiful."

Blake huffed. "To you, maybe. I'm the one about to get a frequent-patient card for the ER."

She had to smile. Leave it to Blake to bring some levity into the situation. "I mean, they've all been halfhearted. Running you off the road, the Mountain Dew, the pallets— they seem like the kind of attempts someone would choose if they wanted to be able to say they'd tried to kill you, but hadn't succeeded. Those attempts gave you a solid chance of surviving."

Max and Blake didn't look convinced.

"That peanut move he made on Caroline wasn't halfhearted." Max shook his head.

"Wasn't it? He could have assumed she would eat it in the presence of others, people who could help her—likely at work, a place where there are multiple EpiPens on hand."

"I don't know, Z."

"I'm not saying the attempts weren't legit, but they don't

fit the way the Kovacs operate. If they want you dead, you die. You don't get your Mountain Dew poisoned. You get an injection of something that does the job. You don't have pallets fall on you. You get jumped in an alley and it looks like a robbery gone bad."

She pointed to the waterfall. "Even this morning. He waited. Do you see? He watched Blake for fifteen minutes. Anytime in that fifteen minutes, he could have shot him, or rushed him and knocked him over, and there would have been nothing we could do about it."

"Are you saying he waited for you to get there? Because that's bad. That means he knows you're not a quality consultant." Max shifted on the ground. "What if he knows who you really are, and your history with the Kovac family?"

"There is no way he could know who I am, remember?"

She looked at Blake. "After the Thompsons died, the person I was died, too. Uncle Frank worked up a brand-new identity. The public record for Heidi Zimmerman barely exists until I entered Virginia Tech. There's no way the Kovacs could have made the connection."

She turned back to Max. "But that's not where I was going with this. Hear me out." She hopped up and walked over to where she'd first seen Markos.

"Markos stood here, watching. He had a gun and a baseball bat. He kept shaking his head and there was no bloodlust. There was nothing but sadness on his face. I had a perfect view. This was a man doing what he had to do, not what he wanted to do."

She shifted her position again. "Then, after I'd shot him, he lay here, watching us. He took his time." She tried to move her hand at the same pace Markos did in her memory. "He showed me his hand. If he'd acted quickly, he could have blown all three of us to bits before we had a chance to run, but he didn't. It's like he wanted us to have time to get out of the way."

She could tell Blake and Max were following her logic now.

"Guys," she said, "I'm not saying Kovac wasn't up to his neck in all of this, but I am saying there is no way he was calling the shots. He hasn't been in charge. He's been the foot soldier. And whoever is running this show is still out there. And they aren't done."

FIFTEEN

Blake didn't see why this was a shock. "I thought we knew he wasn't in charge. You said the Kovac family was behind it."

"Big picture, yes. But the day in, day out operation should have been his all the way. Like a test. The younger family members try their hands at all sorts of criminal activities as a way to prove themselves, but it's compartmentalized. The family wouldn't risk being exposed," Max said.

"And if any of the other Kovacs had been calling the shots, you'd be dead." Heidi said the words with such matter-of-fact certainty it chilled Blake to his core. With what he now knew about Heidi's history, he couldn't doubt she knew what she was talking about.

"How much danger is my family in?"

Max and Heidi shared a long look. He'd seen it before. They'd been partners so long, they had a way of communicating without words. He didn't like it. If he wanted to be fair, he'd admit that he didn't like it because it made him jealous. Because he wanted to know her that well. And he didn't want anyone else to.

He was in no mood to be fair. "Would you two stop talking without talking and tell me what you're thinking?"

Max sighed. "We'll increase security. The Kovacs don't play fair. Any member of your family—pretty much anyone you care about—could be a target. Your entire family will need to stay close and cooperate with our agents fully. We wouldn't want anyone wandering off into the woods and making themselves a prime target, now, would we?"

Blake raised his hands in mock surrender. "Hey, I didn't realize it would be dangerous. I needed to think and…" He caught Heidi's eye, caught the lift of her eyebrow, caught the flicker of understanding. Maybe they'd starting talking without talking, too.

He liked that.

Max didn't seem to notice. "I get it. But you know what's going on and you still didn't think this would be a problem."

"I've been coming up here on Saturday mornings for years." Since Lana left. When Maggie was a baby his trips to the rock had helped him hold on to his sanity.

Heidi and Max looked at each other.

And there they went again. "What did I say?"

Heidi's face wrinkled in confusion. She was so cute when she was puzzling over something. "You come up here every Saturday?"

"Usually."

"How did I not know this?" Heidi frowned at him. Interesting. Was she upset about not knowing because of a professional concern, or a personal one?

"What do you do with Maggie?" Max asked.

"Maggie goes to one set of grandparents or the other most Friday nights. I get up around five and come up here for an hour, then I go back and start my day."

"I still don't understand…"

"What?"

"Why didn't I know?"

"I didn't realize I needed to run my daily schedule past you."

"You don't."

Ha. Her expression said something different.

Max placed a hand on Heidi's arm. "What we're trying to figure out is why we didn't know and Markos did."

Heidi leaned toward him. "Have you mentioned this routine to friends, coworkers? Is it reasonable to think Markos would have known you make this a habit?"

"It's not a secret. In fact, we talked about it the other day. One of the guys said he never goes anywhere without his phone and I said I always come up here on Saturday without mine. This is where I unplug, unwind. Mark could have overheard."

"You come up here without your phone?" He could hear fear in Heidi's words.

"I did before you came along. Since I met you, I keep my phone with me at all times."

Heidi let out a sigh. "Good. Please don't go anywhere without your phone. Ever."

"Worried you might lose me?"

He meant the words as a joke, but the worry in Heidi's face told him she hadn't taken it that way.

"Hey." He reached for her arm and she let him pull her toward him. He didn't wrap his arms around her, although he wanted to. Instead, he rubbed her arms from shoulder to elbow. "You are stuck with me for life. Get used to it."

"Whoa, dude." Max stepped away with a laugh. "Might not be the best time to propose." He walked off chuckling. Heidi laughed, but her eyes narrowed as she looked into his.

"We've discussed this before. The more you get to know me, the more you'll wish you could get away. When this case is over, you'll be so relieved to be rid of me you won't know how to handle it."

He squeezed her biceps and pulled her closer. "I will never want to be rid of you, so quit trying to scare me off. It hasn't worked yet and it's not going to."

She stood a foot away, eyes wide and vulnerable, mouth

so kissable. All he'd have to do is take one step to close the distance—

"Z, get over here!"

One of the agents who'd descended on his mountain called to her. "Look at this."

Blake followed. At some point, he assumed they would make him leave, but as long as he could stay close to Heidi, he would.

"What do you make of this?" The agent pointed to a melted and scorched piece of plastic.

Heidi knelt beside it. "Got some clean gloves?"

The agent pulled a pair from his jacket. She put one on, and used the other to pick up the plastic. A few wires protruded. The look on her face told him she did not like what she was seeing.

"Looks like a cell-phone trigger to me," Heidi said.

"Me, too, but I can't figure out how it would have worked. He would have had to have the number open and be ready to hit the send button, but you said he touched his jacket and blew up."

"That's what happened."

"So—"

"He didn't trigger the bomb. Someone else did."

Three hours later, Heidi sat on a mossy log several hundred yards from the scene. She would have preferred to sun herself like the lizard she'd seen earlier on Blake's rock. Cute little thing, soaking up the rays. Oblivious to the tragedy unfolding all around him.

She dropped her head into her trembling hands. She'd almost lost him. The Kovacs had tried to take someone she loved. Again. And there was no denying that Blake was someone she loved. She couldn't take back her feelings, even if she could never act on them. Blake Harrison had captured her heart and now the Kovacs had a new weapon in their arsenal.

Because she would do anything to keep Blake Harrison alive.

Even if she couldn't have him, she would need to know he was alive and happy. She needed to know places like HPI existed, where good people got up and went to work and made quality products and paid their employees an honest living and delivered what they promised to their customers.

If the Kovacs thought she was going to sit back and watch them destroy another family, they'd messed with the wrong girl.

Again.

She'd get those—

"Hey."

She started at the voice. "Uncle Frank? What are you doing here?"

"Heard you got in a shoot-out, threw in a little hand-to-hand combat, a suicide bombing and then caught on fire. Seemed like it might be worth a personal visit." He gave her a grim smile. "How you holding up?"

"I'm going to catch them."

"Not what I asked you."

"That's my answer."

He shook his head. "You are the most stubborn woman alive."

"I've already had my freak-out, if that's what you want to know. My clothes caught on fire, and I think my hair is singed. I smell like smoke and flesh. I'm starving, and the more I think about it, the more I think I just watched a man get killed."

"You don't think he detonated the bomb himself?"

"I think he knew what would happen and I think he was buying us time to get away from him, but I think someone else detonated it."

"Then why didn't they act sooner and finish you off?"

"I'm guessing they had a cell-phone trigger and they had ears but no eyes."

Uncle Frank leaned against a nearby tree. "I'm worried about you."

He should have been, but she couldn't tell him that. She focused on keeping her face and eyes clear of any of the telltale emotions roiling inside. Her anger at the Kovacs. Her frustration at Markos. And especially the troubling and intense emotions surging through her with every thought of Blake. Emotions she'd have to put aside until this was over.

Uncle Frank pulled out his phone. "TacOps says the Kovac residence remains still. I've already ordered a team to go in and figure out what he was up to."

"There's no telling what they'll find."

"I agree. If the wife is alive, she'll be taken into protective custody, regardless of whether or not she wants to be. We have to question Mrs. Kovac, and I want you to do it."

"Me?" Heidi had run her share of interrogations, but she'd expected Uncle Frank would want to talk to Katarina Kovac himself. Or at least to keep Heidi from talking to her.

"I know you have a lot riding on this." He threw a look in Blake's direction and Heidi pretended not to notice the implication. "But you're the best one for it. You aren't needed up here anymore. Get down the mountain, clean up and prepare to talk to her. I'll let you know when the team enters their home."

"Thanks."

"And, Heidi?"

"Yes, sir."

"I'm glad you're okay."

Heidi stood in her bathroom and pulled her hair over her shoulder. Yep. Singed. As bad as this day had been, at least her hair hadn't burned off this time.

Although it had been close enough.

"Z!"

Max's yell came from downstairs. Blake must have let him in. Or maybe he'd let himself in.

"One second." So much for cleaning up. She'd have to settle for fresh clothes. She ducked into the bedroom and pulled a clean tank top over her head, then grabbed a sweater out of her dresser before dashing down the stairs.

She noted the surprised look on Max's face, and the appreciative uptick of Blake's brows. She kept giving him opportunities to be disgusted by the sight of her, but he kept refusing to be disgusted. If anything, he seemed more interested than ever.

"Katarina Kovac is in the wind." Max's words yanked her thoughts back to the case.

"What?"

"Either she's dead or she's been in on it from the beginning. If she's bolted, she'll be in the Caribbean or Europe by tomorrow."

Heidi looked at Max. "Or?"

Max grimaced. "I don't think it's safe to rule anything out right now."

"Rule out what?" Blake's eyes darted between her face and Max's.

"That maybe she plans to finish the job," Max said.

"Or that she's been in charge from the beginning." Heidi's brain spun with the implications. "We need to rethink everything."

"I'm going back up the mountain to check on the forensics guys," Max said. "Let me know if you find anything."

Heidi pulled the sofa back from the coffee table and pried two floorboards loose, revealing a safe.

"When did you install that?" Blake pointed to the floor.

"I didn't." She opened the safe. "I found it my second day here when I dropped a pen under the sofa. Noticed the loose boards and found this little hidey-hole." She pulled out a stack of files. "You didn't know about it?"

"No."

"When this is over, we'll have to get the TacOps guys to come scan the floors and walls. Who knows what your grandparents stashed around here?" She pulled out the last file and Blake slid the sofa back over the opening. "For now, let's figure out what the Kovacs were up to."

Five hours and a large meat-lovers' pizza later, Heidi tossed a stack of invoices on the sofa. "These can go in the 'appear to be harmless' column."

The "appear to be harmless" column was long.

The "might be something" column included two shipments lost in a trucking accident a week before Heidi's arrival at HPI and one order from a client who had paid but never provided delivery information.

That one had to mean something—they just weren't sure what. Blake had been poring over the file for the past fifteen minutes while finishing off another slice of pizza and the last of a two-liter Coke. Heidi couldn't resist watching him. He had an array of papers on his left and held a spreadsheet in his right hand.

Father, help me.

She loved him.

She shouldn't. He deserved someone who didn't have her memories. Someone who worried more about fashion trends than political climates. Someone who lived here and wanted to live here forever.

Well, the last part applied, but it didn't matter. She had a job to do that would take her away from here. Did he realize it was all ending? That the days of Saturday tea parties and Sunday church and Monday mornings in the office were already over?

He glanced up and caught her staring. A slow smile tinged with sadness spread across his face. He knew.

He put the papers down and leaned forward, resting his

elbows on his knees and clasping his hands. "You're distracting me."

She should be sorry.

She wasn't.

His Adam's apple bobbed and his thumbs made small circles around each other. Was he going to acknowledge what they both knew? What would she do if he did?

His mouth twisted into a grimace and he picked up the spreadsheet again. "I think there's something here." He pointed to a line he'd highlighted in yellow. "What if this order was never real? What if the company that ordered it didn't exist? What if the Kovacs ordered these bottles?"

"Wouldn't you have noticed?"

"Not necessarily."

"No way. You know everything going on."

He acknowledged the truth of her remark with a wink and a shrug before he handed her the spreadsheet. "Look at the order date."

"October 4?"

"We were on a cruise."

"What? Who?" In the months she'd been here, she'd never seen a single day of operation where at least one of the Harrisons hadn't been present.

"All of us. Me, Maggie, Mom, Dad and Caroline."

"Why?"

"Caroline's thirtieth birthday. It was all she wanted. For the entire family to go on a vacation and not worry about the plant for once."

"Who would have taken the order?"

"The salesmen put the orders in, but it wouldn't be too hard for anyone with basic knowledge of our process to put in a fake order." He tapped the sheet. "This is the order we kept messing up. I think we went through four off-quality batches before we nailed it."

"And the off-quality batches would have been packed up to go to reclamation."

"Exactly. He could have taken them."

"Why?"

He sighed. "No idea."

Heidi wanted to scream. There was something here.

Heidi's phone buzzed. "Zimmerman."

"Z, it's Richards. We're ready to go in. Max said you'd want to be here."

"We'll be there in fifteen minutes."

Blake raised his eyebrows. "We're going somewhere?"

"The Kovacs' house. TacOps is going in." He didn't look as excited as she'd expected. "You don't have to go…"

"I *want* to go, but I'm surprised you're letting me."

"I shouldn't. You're still recovering from a concussion and you should be resting. But I doubt you'd get much rest while I'm gone, and I'm hoping we'll find something you'll be able to make sense of."

They drove to the Kovacs' in silence and found the house shrouded in darkness.

"I thought there'd be spotlights and dogs. Maybe a helicopter circling," Blake said.

"Not TacOps style. We want to enter and get out without anyone noticing. If possible." She could see teams stationed at three corners of the house and she knew another was at the back. Two vans parked one hundred feet from the house would be the command centers.

An unusually obvious showing for TacOps, but they'd staged an accident and had a detour set up to prevent any civilian traffic from passing the driveway. The Kovacs' house sat off the road on a wooded lot, increasing their chances no one would ever know they'd been here.

They walked to the van and found Richards waiting. "Glad you're here." He pointed to Blake. "I'm fine with him coming in, but I want you both to wait until I give the all-clear."

Heidi nodded. "Be careful."

She stepped back as Richards gave his final instructions to the teams. Blake watched everything with a calm expression, but she knew him well enough to know he was bursting with questions.

She nodded at him and he followed her away from the vans. She handed him a pair of night-vision goggles. "If you look you'll be able to see the teams. The dogs you mentioned have already done the first step. They've checked for explosive residues. The teams at the house are visually checking for trip wires or anything indicating the house is booby-trapped. Once they give the okay, the teams will enter through the front and back doors simultaneously."

The doors opened and Blake sucked in a breath.

"Now the waiting begins. You'll want to drop the goggles. They'll turn the lights on in a few minutes."

"Do I want to know how dangerous this is?" Blake handed her the goggles.

"No."

"And you used to do this?"

"Yes."

He shook his head. "How did you do it?"

"You rely on your training. And you pray, a lot."

The lights came on in the house and agents streamed in and out. Five excruciating minutes passed before a flurry of activity and sounds pierced the night silence. Agents poured out of every door. Richards stepped onto the front porch and yelled, "Yo, Z! Get over here!"

SIXTEEN

Blake jogged beside Heidi. At Richards's call, her features had hardened into an expression he'd come to recognize as her "this is serious" look.

They had to pull up before they reached the house as two agents strung a roll of caution tape in front of them. "I wouldn't go any closer, ma'am," one of the agents said.

Richards ducked under the tape. "He's right about that," he said.

"What did you find?"

"Nothing."

"Why the hasty retreat?"

"The new dog alerted."

"What new dog?"

"Joined us last week. Been getting specialized training. I'm not sure I believe he can do what they claim, but his handler believes—"

Even in the predawn light, Blake saw the color drain from Heidi's face. "Can he tell what it is?"

"I have a bioterror team scrambling, but the handler says anthrax."

Heidi took a step back. "No, this doesn't make sense."

Richards said something, but Blake didn't catch his words. He kept replaying "anthrax" over and over in his mind. Had they been exposed? Maggie? His family? Could they get vaccinated? Would that even help?

Someone yelled for Richards and he excused himself. Heidi turned to him. "We'll have the dog sweep the plant and all your homes. If he alerts to anything, we'll vaccinate your family and anyone who has stepped into the plant in the last three months," she said. "There've been no outbreaks, so whatever they were planning to do, they haven't done it yet. At least, I don't think they have."

"Will vaccinations work?"

"I don't know." Heidi ran both hands through her curls as Max jogged up.

"You've heard."

"Yeah."

"Think the dog can do that?"

"We can't risk it either way. Not until we have a confirmed analysis."

"What on earth are the Kovacs doing with anthrax?"

"Something bad. Something very bad."

It took until 3:00 a.m. for HPI and the Harrisons' homes to be declared anthrax-free. Blake hoped that dog was as good as they said. The handler was confident. So was Heidi. And as Heidi pointed out, if the dog couldn't find it, nothing else would.

It looked like the Kovacs' anthrax plans had been thwarted. Still, Blake couldn't let himself relax. It didn't *feel* over yet.

When the last FBI agent drove away, Heidi turned to Blake. "What time will Maggie be back tomorrow?"

"Four o'clock."

She gave him a small smile. "Good. You need to get some sleep."

"So do you," he said as he pulled her arm into his and turned their steps toward the car. "What happens tomorrow?"

"Somewhere above my pay grade, people are deciding

how to spin this. By tomorrow, they will have a story and a plan for implementation. My guess is they will keep this hushed up. No media coverage. No 'we stopped an anthrax plot' press conference."

"Why not?"

"Because we haven't. Somewhere, the Kovacs have a supply of anthrax. At least, if that dog knows his stuff, they do. They have it, and they intended to distribute it in some way. But we can't prove it. Rather than make a big show, we keep what we know to ourselves. If the dog hadn't alerted, we wouldn't have known there was anthrax in the house for days, maybe not ever."

"Instead of letting on you know about it, you let them think they've gotten away with it?"

"Exactly. I'm not sure when it will all be resolved."

He couldn't deny that anything that kept her here a few days longer was fine with him. He knew every time they took a step closer to stopping the Kovacs' plot he also took one step closer to telling her goodbye, and there was no way he was going to miss out on any of the dwindling moments they had left.

He'd had a lot of time to think today. From his early-morning communion with God, to the adrenaline rush of the confrontation with Mark, to the intense emotions that had flooded through him as he'd held Heidi while she sobbed, to the quiet moments as he tried to stay out of the way while Heidi did her job.

He'd been asking God why for a long time. Years. Why had God allowed him to fall in love with a woman who He'd known would someday leave him and their daughter? Why had God allowed him to hire a mobster? Why would He allow him to fall in love with Heidi—a woman he could never have?

Because he knew he loved her. His heart belonged with hers. Forever.

God hadn't answered his question yet, maybe He never would. Blake had the sense God wasn't asking him to understand everything, just to trust.

That's what he was going to do.

Trust that God already had all the information and He'd share it when he needed to know.

Heidi pulled into Blake's driveway and put the car in Park. When she turned to him, he brushed her cheek with his thumb. What he wouldn't give to be able to pull her toward him. Instead, he said, "Call me if anything happens?"

"Promise."

Heidi kicked her shoes off and slid between her sheets. Her last conscious thought was that she should set her alarm.

She didn't.

When she woke, the sun shone through the bedroom window at an odd angle. She'd never noticed it being in her eyes like this before. She rubbed her face. Where was her phone? She blinked a few times and spotted it on the pillow.

It was 10:47 a.m.

She groaned. How had she slept so late? Why hadn't anyone called her? The biggest case she'd ever been a part of and she'd slept the morning away?

Her phone vibrated in her hand. A text from Max.

Call me when you wake up. No news.

Maybe the sleep hadn't been such a bad idea. She stumbled into the bathroom, wishing she'd showered last night. She smelled like smoke, dirt, sweat and burned hair.

A hot shower and a cup of tea later, she called Max.

"Glad you decided to join us in the land of the living," he said.

She yawned. "Sorry. Where are we?"

"Pretty much where we were last night."

She'd hoped for more, but she wasn't surprised. This was real life, not a TV drama. Lab results and forensic searches required more than fifteen minutes to be completed.

"What do you want to do next?"

Heidi ripped into a granola bar and took a bite. "I think we have to go back to HPI. We may—"

Her door rattled as someone pounded on it. She dropped the granola bar and pulled her weapon from its standard spot at her lower back.

"Heidi! Are you in there?"

"Blake?"

"Come on, Heidi. I'm not under duress. Open the door."

"Hang on, Max," she said into the phone as she eased the door open.

Blake stood a few steps back on the porch, hands raised in a mock surrender. "We need to come up with a safe word, don't we?"

"Yeah." But what would be the point when it was almost over?

"I have a hunch about what Mark was up to. I need to check something at the plant. Want to come?"

"Want to? I don't want you going alone, that's for sure."

"Then come on."

Heidi ended her call with Max as she pulled on her shoes. "I'll drive," she said.

"Nope. It's been five days. I'm good."

Had it really been five days? In some ways it felt like this week had been one endless day.

She grabbed a ball cap, but Blake caught it before she could cram it on her head. "Don't."

"My hair—"

"Is adorable. I like it all wet and extra curly. Leave it."

Had that concussion finally caught up to him? He

grabbed her hand and pulled her to his car, opening the passenger-side door for her.

"You hate my hair."

"No, I don't." He lifted a few damp curls and let them slide through his fingers. "I love it."

He winked and closed her door.

What on earth? Was it possible she'd found a man who not only wasn't repulsed by the scars covering her body, but who also didn't mind the curly mess calling her head home? It would figure the one man who could handle all of her was also a man she could never have. He liked her, but he'd never act on it.

He settled into the driver's seat. "What's with you and your hair?"

"What do you mean?"

"You don't straighten it, but you have a chip on your shoulder about it."

"Let's talk about your hunch."

"After you tell me about your hair."

She stared out the window. "I don't mean to have a chip on my shoulder about it."

"Maybe I used the wrong phrase. You seem sensitive about it."

What did it matter anymore? She might as well tell him. "My freshman year at Virginia Tech was tough. I was very much alone, and…I think the term is *emotionally fragile*."

She rubbed her hands on her jeans before she dove back in. "I met this guy in a chemistry class. Thought we were friends. When he asked me out, I was thrilled. Then he started making little remarks about my hair and my clothes. I straightened my hair because he liked it better straight."

"Idiot," Blake said under his breath.

"Who? Him or me?"

"Him."

"True, but I was an idiot for letting him control me."

"You were, what, eighteen? No family? Having gone through what you'd been through? You just wanted to be liked—he's the one who took advantage."

"Thank you for that. At the time, it seemed reasonable. Now it seems ridiculous. Anyway, when he started suggesting I wear shorts or tank tops, I told him about the burns. He said he didn't care."

She could still see his face. Even without any training, she'd recognized the lie.

"But he did," Blake said, and Heidi could hear the undercurrent of fury in his words.

"He did," she agreed.

"Does this guy still waste oxygen?"

Man, it felt good to be protected. "He does. Married a girl with a perfect pedigree and the perfect body to match. Divorced her a few years ago and married another one, ten years younger."

"Some men are morons, Heidi."

"With a few obvious exceptions," she said, trying to infuse some teasing into the conversation.

"No, I'm a moron, too. If I'd had any sense, I'd have kissed you three months ago."

Heidi sucked in a breath.

"And I'd have been kissing you every day since then. Now I'm out of time."

Heidi tried to swallow but her mouth had gone dry. Why was he saying this? Every part of her wanted to tell him she wished he'd been kissing her every day, too. But he deserved more than she could give. "You'll be better off without me."

"No. I won't."

She couldn't think of what to say. He hadn't said he loved her. He hadn't asked her to stay. But he'd put it out there, that the feelings she'd sensed simmering under the surface were real. She watched his face as they pulled into the empty HPI lot. He put the car into Park and pulled the keys from the ignition.

When he looked at her, every reason she had for stopping this from going any further left her mind and all she could think of was how much she wanted him to hold her and tell her they'd figure it out.

The honking horn to her right jerked her attention to her surroundings.

Max.

She'd strangle him as soon as she got the chance.

Blake gave her a rueful smile and whispered, "Later?"

Yes. Later.

Blake couldn't believe he'd done that.

He'd promised himself he wouldn't. He had no right to make any claim on her. To try to make anything work between them. He should let her go.

But when she'd opened the door with her bare feet and her wet hair and her gun in her hand, he'd been undone. This woman didn't fit anything he'd ever thought he'd want or need, but it turned out she was everything he needed and the only one he would ever want.

And he did want her.

If Max hadn't pulled up when he had, he would have told her he loved her. Would have shown her. His timing stunk.

How many romantic moments had they shared? Long chats on the porch swing, walks in the woods, even late nights around the coffee table with a pizza and a carton of ice cream. And he had to go and attempt to tell her he loved her while driving in the car on their way to uncover a criminal plot?

Brilliant.

They got out of the car and Max joined them. "What's the deal?"

"You'll have to ask Blake."

They both looked at him.

"It may be nothing, but I keep thinking about what we know they've done. They've messed up a few shipments and may have created false orders. It got me thinking. What if they were trying to do something to shipments that would never reach the customers?"

Heidi and Max exchanged blank looks.

"What if they were trying to perfect a way to contaminate bottles, but they didn't want those bottles to get out until they were ready? They would need to test it on bottles that were never going to reach the customer because they didn't meet our quality specifications."

He could see Heidi had caught on.

"You think all those off-quality batches were intentional, to hide something else?"

"Maybe, and I think I might know where they were doing it."

"Where?"

"The blower."

Recognition swept across Heidi's face and he knew she was thinking the same thing he was.

"The blower you were working on my first day here?"

"The same."

"Why that one?" Max wasn't following.

"It's given us fits, and it has enough nooks and crannies for Mark to hide something without anyone noticing. I want to check it out. I'll take it apart bolt by bolt if I have to."

Heidi nodded. "It's plausible."

Max shrugged. "I have no idea what you're talking about, but I'm game."

They walked through the silent plant floor and he fought the urge to reach for Heidi's hand. He pulled out his flashlight as he walked around the new blower several times.

"See anything?" Heidi asked from the other side of the equipment.

"No, do you?" With her memory and familiarity with the process, she'd spot anything out of the ordinary.

She shook her head. Blake shimmied under the front end of the machine. Everything looked different from the back side. Wires filled with air, oil and coolant coiled in a maze of colors and sizes. If he didn't find anything obvious, he'd need to trace each one. He scooted farther down the line, slowly scanning each section with his flashlight.

Nothing.

He went as far as he could before a support column blocked his path, forcing him to slide back out. Max and Heidi eyed him with expectant looks on their faces. At his shrug, Max's face fell, but Heidi nodded her encouragement, her face full of hope and belief. He dove back under and made his way toward the end.

What was that?

He edged closer toward the brick-shaped object. Wrapped in black electrical tape, it blended in to several of the other wire bundles, but this one had a small tube coming out of one end, and nothing going in as far as he could tell.

He wiggled his way back out and then back to the same spot on the front side of the equipment.

"There." He pointed into the space the bottles followed after they'd been blown into shape but before they'd been turned on their end. A tiny nozzle.

Heidi traced the beam of his flashlight with her finger, but stopped short of touching the nozzle. "This?"

"Yes. That's not supposed to be here."

Heidi's face wrinkled in confusion. "Blake, that nozzle's been here as long as I have."

"Are you sure?"

Max rolled his eyes. "Dude, if she says she's seen it..."

"I know, I know, but you would have noticed this?"

"Yes. I did notice it. I didn't crawl underneath the blower like you did. I assumed it was an additional nozzle you used in specialty applications. In fact, I'm pretty sure I read something about it in the manual."

This woman would never cease to amaze him. He had no doubt she could give him the page number where she'd read it, but she was trying not to come across as a know-it-all. "Yes, they do come as an add-on. We didn't anticipate needing them anytime in the future, and if we do need them later, we discussed—"

Oh, no.

"Discussed what?"

"When we were working through the specifications on this line, Mark came with me when we went to see this model in action. We had a whole conversation about how easy it would be to install additional nozzles if we needed them."

Max whistled. "Did the dog sweep this area last night?"

"He did."

"So they haven't used it yet."

"I don't think so."

"I'm going to have the forensics guys come back to swab this stuff to be sure."

"I don't think that's a bad idea, but you know we thoroughly clean the lines in between each run. If they ever had used it, we couldn't expect to find more than a trace."

"It wouldn't take more than a trace of anthrax to kill someone."

SEVENTEEN

Heidi couldn't believe it. It had been here all along. One lonely little nozzle with a tip the size of a dime, sitting in plain sight.

If you were looking.

And she had been. She'd looked a thousand times. Why had she assumed it was nothing?

Markos was dead and she couldn't shake the suspicion that he'd not been as committed to this scheme as the family expected him to be. Had his own family killed him the way they'd killed Joe? Could he have been looking for a way out? If she'd picked up on his wavering earlier and approached him, would he have given them all they needed to take the entire family down?

She rubbed her hands over her face. When she looked up, Max had his phone to his ear.

"You'll have to go outside if you want to get decent reception."

He nodded and mouthed, "Lab," as he went toward the door.

"Where's he headed?"

"He'll be checking to see if there are any lab results yet, and then he'll line somebody up to come get this little present Markos has left for us."

"I can get it out of there, no problem."

"No!"

Blake held up his hands. "Sorry."

"I'm sorry I yelled. But we don't know what's in it and we don't know if they booby-trapped it to keep it from being removed."

"Ah. Good point."

Max returned and she knew he had bad news from his demeanor. She rested her hand on Blake's arm, for his benefit or hers, she couldn't say. "What is it?" she asked. At her words, Blake leaned closer and put his hand over hers.

Max narrowed his eyes at her and she knew he hadn't missed the way she and Blake were standing.

"The lab results aren't definite yet, but with the way this stuff is growing, they are pretty sure the dog was right."

Heidi's mind raced. The implications were horrible. "They wanted to contaminate the containers with anthrax. It's not a bad plan. I mean, it's pure evil, but it's genius. They contaminate water bottles or food containers. With this system in place, they could pick and choose which runs they wanted to contaminate."

"What would their success rate be?"

"The anthrax spores would sit in the containers all chilled out until someone drank or ate from them. Then they'd get comfy in a nice warm stomach and they'd go active. What makes it so perfect is that the success rate won't be one hundred percent. Not all the spores will go active before they are expelled from the body. Some people won't get sick, some will. You ship all over the country, so random anthrax outbreaks start popping up in various places. It would be difficult to trace and that would make it almost impossible to stop."

Heidi looked at Blake, then Max, hoping one of them would stop her. Tell her she'd gotten it all wrong. But they didn't, so she continued.

"The Kovacs get this bright idea, but they need to get

someone on the inside. Markos may have applied for positions all over the country, but this is where he got the job. They would have been ecstatic. He settles into the job, learns the ropes, starts experimenting with different ways to plant the anthrax."

Max picked up. "Then you start following him around, Blake, asking lots of questions, checking up on him when you notice the quality issues in his batches. He, or maybe the senior Kovacs, decide they've invested too much in this to fail and they try to take you out. You're the real problem."

"I like the theory," Heidi said, "but what about the attack on Caroline?"

Max started to say something a few times, then shrugged. "No idea. We'll come back to that. What I want to know is what were they waiting on? If they've got the anthrax and they've got the method, why not use it?"

"Maybe they had a limited supply and wanted to get the biggest bang for their buck?"

"The ballpark bottles." Blake and Heidi spoke in unison. Blake grinned at her. Yes, definitely starting to think alike.

She turned to Max. "They would have been perfect. National distribution, potential for thousands if not millions of cases, all spread out over months and months."

Heidi pointed at Blake. "I guess we know why Markos wanted you out of the picture."

"What do you mean?"

"Anytime anything happens with this blower, they call you. It's your project. You're the expert. He couldn't risk you catching on to what he was doing and noticing this extra nozzle in place. My guess is the Kovacs have a lot riding on this."

Heidi ran her hands through her hair.

"Of course!"

"What?"

"The Kovacs. They have stakes in multiple health care

and security companies. A few months ago, I ran across some sketchy evidence indicating they may have a shell company that owns a controlling share in one of the anthrax vaccine producers. An anthrax scare would send stock prices soaring. They'd make a fortune."

Max joined in. "And if they were able to trigger the scare and then get back out of it without anyone knowing how they did it..."

"They'd be able to do it again."

"Or sell the technology to the highest bidder."

Most of the FBI agents had already headed out, either to their homes or to other pressing cases. The handful of agents remaining were coordinating with local officials in their efforts to locate Katarina Kovac.

Heidi caught one of the forensic techs who hadn't left yet and asked her to take samples from the blower before she left town. Heidi and Blake had hung out at HPI until the forensic tech had what she needed and then they headed home.

Home? The cabin was as much of a home as Heidi had ever had. Homesickness engulfed her. Everything was ending and her heart throbbed at the coming goodbyes.

Blake threw the car in Park and winked at her. "Good job today, Special Agent Zimmerman." His words pulled Heidi back into the present.

"It was your idea," she said as she stepped from the car. "You're the one who found the sabotage. Congrats. You've foiled your first criminal plot. How does it feel?"

She'd meant the words to be teasing and light, but Blake didn't smile. He shook his head and sighed. "When will you be leaving?"

Heidi studied the ground and fiddled with her phone. She didn't look up, even as he stepped closer. "Soon. I'll stay for a week or two to maintain my cover. Like I said, we'll be trying to keep this quiet in the media, so it's best if I don't do anything that will raise any questions. I'll be here for a few more days, and then go. I mean, that's the plan. I'm due some vacation time, so I don't have to pack my bags and rush off, but… Soon."

She needed to go inside, to get away from him before she couldn't take it anymore. She turned, but his hand closed around her arm and he pulled her against him in one quick motion. She knew she should pull away. She didn't. His hand had found her waist, and while his arms were wrapping around her, his touch was gentle and she knew all she'd have to do was take one step back and he would release her.

She leaned in.

His lips found hers, gentle and soft at first, then more insistent and she knew he was feeling everything she was. Love, beautiful and precious, and in their case, impossible.

At some point, she pulled back enough to breathe and rested her head on his chest. He squeezed her close. "What are we going to do?" He whispered the words into her hair and she looked up. Before she could answer, he kissed her again. His hands found their way into her hair, then down her back. He pulled away this time, his chest heaving.

"You were saying?"

"I can't remember."

She could barely remember her own name. She didn't care about organized-crime families or anthrax plots or national security.

All right, that wasn't true—she cared, but she just couldn't care enough to force herself to move out of Blake's arms.

The sound of wheels on pavement forced her to step back.

"The Petersons are bringing Maggie home," Blake said.

The car idled for a brief moment. Maggie blew kisses at her grandparents and then raced toward Blake's waiting arms. He buried his face in her hair and squeezed her tight until she squirmed and squealed to be released.

When he set her down, Maggie ran to Heidi. "I missed you, Miss Heidi!"

Those five words threatened the fragile grip Heidi had on her emotions. She knelt beside her and gave her a hug. "I missed you, too, sweetheart." She couldn't look at Blake.

How would she ever say goodbye to this child and continue to function? Would she be able to continue to breathe when her heart had been left behind in the mountains of North Carolina?

"I haven't seen you in days and days, Miss Heidi. Where have you been?"

"I've been working, sweetie."

Maggie furrowed her brow. "Which job?"

"What?"

"Your real job, or your FBI job?"

How on earth? What could she say? Blake looked as shocked as she was. "Maggie, what do you mean?"

Maggie rolled her eyes and shook her head. "Miss Heidi." She let out a little huff. "I do live here." Only a five-year-old could be so adorable while trying to be patronizing.

Blake's phone buzzed. "It's Dad," he said. Blake had been giving him hourly updates via text.

Heidi knew Jeffrey and Eleanor were frustrated to be so far removed from the action, but as sorry as she was for the loss of Jeffrey's cousin, she was thankful they'd been out of the picture for this weekend's drama.

Heidi smiled at Blake. "Why don't I take Maggie for a walk. We'll have a chat about my job, and you can go talk to your dad."

Blake caught on fast. "I think that's a great idea. Do you want a jacket? It's getting chilly." The sun had begun its descent and the wind had a bite to it.

"I think I'm good. We won't be long."

"Okay," Blake said.

Maggie slid her hand into Heidi's and pulled her toward

the creek that ran behind the Harrisons' home. "What is the FBI, Miss Heidi?"

"What do you think it is? Where did you hear that term?"

"I overheard Papa and Daddy talking. They were whispering. I had to be very still and I couldn't hear everything they said."

Heidi could picture the scene. Blake taking a few moments to fill Jeffrey in on something, carefully keeping his voice down. Never knowing his rambunctious daughter couldn't resist the siren song of a big secret.

"Have you told anybody about the FBI? Talked about it at school?"

"Oh, no," Maggie said. She looked up at Heidi. "I never tell secrets."

"That's good," Heidi said. "It's important to be trustworthy, but part of being trustworthy is not listening in on conversations when you know you aren't supposed to hear them."

Color flooded the little girl's cheeks. "You mean I should have told Daddy I heard him."

Heidi tried not to smile. "Yes, but also that you shouldn't have listened in the first place."

Maggie's shoulders slumped. "I'm sorry."

Heidi squeezed her hand and leaned toward her. "You should tell him when we get back to the house."

"Okay." Her little chin trembled.

Heidi knelt in front of her and took both of her hands. "You know what I think?"

Maggie shook her head.

"I think it takes a brave little girl to admit when she's done something she shouldn't, and to ask forgiveness. And I know for a fact that you are a brave little girl."

Maggie's lips twitched. "I am pretty brave," she said.

"Yes, you are."

Maggie's mouth broke into a wide smile. "Watch this!"

They had reached the creek and Maggie darted to a fallen log laying in the water. Before Heidi could stop her, she danced across and jumped to the other side.

"Fabulous!" Heidi clapped as Maggie hopped around the edge of the water, meandering farther downstream until she slipped out of sight around a large pine. Heidi followed her path.

She rounded the pine, expecting Maggie to come into view, but she was nowhere to be seen. Where had she disappeared to? "Maggie?"

A rustle in the trees. Too big for a squirrel. A deer? If she pulled a gun on Maggie, Blake would never forgive her. She slid her hand to her back, wanting to be prepared, just in case. "Maggie? Come on out, sweetie. This isn't the time for hide-and-seek."

"I may have to disagree with you."

Katarina Kovac eased out from behind the pines.

Maggie stood at her side, eyes wide, tears dripping from her cheeks. "I'm sorry, Miss Heidi."

Heidi forced her feet to stay planted in the soil, even as adrenaline coursed through her. No matter what happened next, Katarina Kovac had crossed into unforgivable territory. Heidi focused on Maggie. Five feet had never seemed so far. "You haven't done anything wrong, Maggie. Absolutely nothing." She turned her attention back to Katarina. "Let her go."

Katarina sneered. "Are you kidding me? This little sweetheart." She pulled Maggie closer. Maggie let out a little squeak. "This is my insurance policy."

"I won't let you take her."

"Don't worry," Katarina said. "You'll be coming, too." Behind Maggie, she flashed a knife. "Why don't you drop that gun into the creek and join us."

"What gun?"

Katarina rolled her eyes. "I'll admit you did a great job

pretending to be a quality engineer, but after Markos's unfortunate accident, it wasn't too hard to figure out who you work for." She waved the knife around. "Drop it."

The gleam in Katarina's eyes frightened Heidi far more than the knife.

She made a show of removing her weapon. She wanted to take Katarina out, but the woman crouched behind Maggie's slight frame, making a shot impossible. "It's been you all along, hasn't it?"

Katarina puffed out her chest. "Please. Markos didn't have enough sense to get out of the rain. No way the family would have trusted him with an assignment like this."

So the family knew.

"Now drop your phone," Katarina said.

Heidi dropped her phone in the creek. "Markos seemed like an intelligent guy to me. He managed to get a job at HPI," Heidi said.

"Only because I coached him through what to say at the interview," she said. Heidi had so many questions, but she didn't want to frighten Maggie any more than she already was. "Why did you decide to take him out of the picture?"

"It wasn't my call." A faint hint of sadness trickled through her words. "But I do what I'm told."

She pointed the knife in Heidi's direction. "Which is what you'd better do. Start walking."

Heidi didn't have a choice. She walked down the creek bank, turning often to see if Maggie was all right. Trying to give her an encouraging smile or a wink each time. She kept her pace slow, both for Maggie's benefit and in the hope that Blake would come looking for them.

Too soon, they broke into a clearing at the back of the HPI parking lot, a beige sedan the only car in sight.

This was it. The best opportunity she'd have. When they got in the car, she might have a chance to get Maggie away from Katarina.

Katarina motioned with the knife. "Get in the car, in the driver's seat. Put both hands on the wheel where I can see them. Don't try anything funny." Over Maggie's head, she pointed to her ear. The meaning was clear. One wrong move on Heidi's part and she'd slice off Maggie's ear.

Heidi's stomach flooded with acid, but she climbed into the car and put both hands on the wheel as instructed. As long as she stayed alive, there was hope.

Father, please help. Help me see how we're going to get out of this.

She watched Katarina. She only needed her to remove the knife from Maggie's neck for a few seconds when she slid her into the car.

She didn't get those seconds. With one hand firmly around Maggie's neck and the other gripping the knife, Katarina urged Maggie into the seat.

Heidi swallowed hard. "I don't have any keys," she said.

"You won't need them." Katarina smiled at her in the rearview mirror.

What was happening? Heidi's arms dropped to her side. No. She had to keep holding on to the steering wheel or Katarina might flip out. Why couldn't she move? She began to tip toward the driver's-side door. Why wouldn't her body respond?

The door opened and Katarina shoved her toward the passenger side. She couldn't prevent her head from smacking against a bag in the seat. Heidi used every ounce of strength she had left to force her eyes to stay open. As Katarina draped the steering wheel in heavy plastic, the truth pierced through her foggy consciousness.

Katarina had booby-trapped her own car. The steering wheel must have been coated with some sort of drug. A drug that had quickly been absorbed by her hands. A drug that had left her helpless to fight back.

"Better life through chemicals, I always say." Katarina's singsong voice was the last thing Heidi heard.

EIGHTEEN

Blake took a sip of Mountain Dew and leaned against his kitchen counter. "That's where we are." He glanced at his watch. It had taken him an hour to explain everything that had happened.

His dad sighed into the phone. "So Mark comes down here, and gets a job with us so he can contaminate containers with anthrax. For some reason, he tries to kill you and Caroline. Several times. And then, when he gets caught he blows himself up, only Heidi doesn't think he did it. She thinks someone else did it, and given that Katarina is missing, either the mysterious someone killed both of them, or Katarina is the one behind it all."

Blake nodded. "Accurate summary."

"So for now, we act like nothing happened? Get back to work and carry on as normal?"

"That's the plan," he said. "They have passive surveillance set up at the Kovacs' house and the local FBI office will be taking over the hunt for Katarina. Max and a couple of agents are staying behind to wrap everything up. And Heidi will stay for a week or so." He didn't want to talk about Heidi with his dad. Not right now. He checked his watch again. "Aren't you about to be late for dinner, Dad?"

"Yes. You be careful. We'll be home on Wednesday."

"Love you, Dad."

"I love you, too, son. I'm so proud of you."

"Thanks, Dad."

Blake disconnected the call and hit the speed-dial button for Heidi's phone. It rang four times and went to voice mail. That was odd. He couldn't remember the last time she hadn't taken a call from him.

Maybe she was on the phone with Max or Frank. Maybe she and Maggie were in deep conversation. They were probably headed back, but he decided to meet them. He didn't know how much more time he would have with Heidi and he didn't want to waste a minute of it.

He expected to find them before he reached the creek. They weren't there.

A vague unease settled in his gut. He quickened his pace as he walked back through the forest toward his house.

He called out for them as he walked. "Heidi! Maggie!"

No reason to panic. Heidi knew this mountain as well as he did. She and Maggie had probably walked farther than they'd planned and it was taking a while for them to get back. They might have even taken a different route and beaten him back to the house.

When he reached his house, he jogged up the steps. "Maggie?" He checked each room. Empty.

"Heidi!" He ran toward the cabin. "Maggie!" He didn't bother knocking on her door. It was locked. He banged on it with his fist. "Heidi! Maggie!" His breath came in gasps as he fumbled with his keys. His hand shook as he slid the key into the door. He raced through the cabin.

They weren't there.

He tried Heidi's phone again. Voice mail. "Heidi, where are you? I'm dying here. Call me."

He ran down the drive, all the way to the road, calling out their names. He scanned the road on either side of the drive.

Would they have come down here? Maybe.

But they would have walked back to the house. Heidi never would have allowed Maggie to walk along the narrow road.

Maybe they'd hiked up to the waterfall. No. Heidi would never take Maggie up there. Not now.

Blake rubbed his temples.

This would be funny in about ten minutes when Heidi and Maggie appeared from some jaunt they'd been on.

It wasn't funny now. He jumped into his car and raced up the mountain to Caroline's. Maggie loved the gazebo at the top of the mountain. So did Heidi. Maybe they'd gone up there.

He slammed the car into Park.

The gazebo sat empty.

He tried to slow his breathing. Tried to stop the thoughts from tumbling over and over in his brain. Missing. Why? Where?

Who?

Father, help me. Help me find them. Help me...

Maybe they'd been circling around each other. He sped back toward his parents' house. Maybe they were watching a movie. That had to be it. The theater room was basically soundproof. They'd probably gotten cold and Maggie had talked Heidi into a movie.

But why wouldn't she answer her phone?

It took five seconds to determine they weren't in the basement.

His phone rang and his heart soared, then crashed. It wasn't Heidi.

An unknown number lit up the phone. He answered. "Yes."

"Hello, Blake," a female voice said.

"Who is this?"

"It doesn't matter, does it? I'm the person who has what you love most in the world."

Blake dropped to his knees.

"Such beautiful blond hair. Such big blue eyes. Such a treasure."

Maggie. Not Maggie. And if they had Maggie, then what had happened to Heidi? "If you hurt her—"

The female voice *tsk*ed in his ear. "Now, Blake. Let's not be difficult. This is the part where you say…" The voice trailed off. Was she prompting him?

"What do you want?"

"Much better. See, this doesn't need to be difficult."

That voice. He knew it from somewhere, but where?

"I'm listening."

"Good. You're going to help me with a project I've been working on. One you have insisted on getting in the way of from the beginning."

It couldn't be, could it? "Katarina?"

Katarina laughed. "Very good, Blake. You're going to meet me at HPI and you're going to ensure my little plan is ready to go with tomorrow morning's production. And, just so we understand each other. You'll be coming alone. You won't be telling any of Heidi's friends about this little conversation. Not if you ever want to see her or your precious Maggie again. Do I make myself clear?"

She had Heidi, too. How on earth could she have managed it? Unless… "How do I know you haven't already killed them?"

He heard a rustling sound. "Daddy?" Maggie's tearful voice unleashed his own tears.

"Yes, baby. Daddy's here. I love you. Are you okay?"

"I'm sorry, Daddy."

"Enough," Katarina said. "You've heard her. She's fine. I'll meet you at the plant entrance in fifteen minutes. Come alone."

The call disconnected.

His world. His whole world. Gone.

What should he do?

What would Heidi do?

He pulled into the parking lot ten minutes later. He still hadn't decided what to do. Calling the police seemed like a bad idea. He could call the FBI, but he had no idea how to get to the people Heidi worked for. He didn't even have Max's number.

He needed time and he didn't have any. Headlights flashed along the drive to the plant. She'd arrived.

All he could do now was let things play out.

And pray.

Father...

He tried. Tried to wrap words around the emotions cartwheeling through his mind and heart. But no words came. He sat in the car, hands clenched around the steering wheel, mind refusing to cooperate. He might die tonight. Maggie might— No. No, he couldn't go there.

He tried again. *Father...*

Nothing.

And yet...a peace began to filter through. Not enough to allay the panic. Not enough for him to feel confident they would all get out of this alive.

But enough to remind him he was not alone. That God heard him. That God was with him, and with Maggie, and Heidi. That He could see them right now and He would give them what they needed to get through whatever was coming.

He'd have preferred a fireball from heaven consuming the car Katarina Kovac sat in, but this peace was enough for him to unclench his hands from the wheel, open the door and face her.

Katarina flashed him a friendly smile as she climbed out of her car. "Thanks for coming, Blake," she said. The friendliness in her voice contrasted with the weapon she pointed in his direction and triggered his sarcasm reflex. As if he'd had a choice. Of course he'd come. What kind of an idiot did she think he was? He had a slew of snide remarks he'd love to make, but this might not be the best time to antagonize the criminal with the gun.

"What do you need me to do, Katarina?"

"Nice. Right to business. Yes, I do like that about you. Come on. In we go." She waved the gun toward the door. A door he'd entered a few short hours ago with Heidi and Max.

Did Katarina realize they knew about the anthrax?

If she didn't, maybe he had a better chance of getting out of this with everyone alive than he'd thought.

"I can't figure out what your plan is, Katarina. Why would you need me?"

"You're going to confirm the installation for me. Be sure it will do what it's supposed to. And then, you're going to go on a vacation. You'll tell your parents the strain has gotten to be too much and you need a break."

Did she really believe they would buy that?

"All I need is the next two days' production runs to go off as planned and these bottles will be hitting the baseball diamonds this summer."

"You'll never get away with this."

She pointed her gun at the door and waited for Blake to unlock it.

"I already have."

He fumbled with the door.

"Come on, I don't have all night."

They went inside and Katarina led him to the line.

"You seem to know your way around pretty well. I didn't think you'd ever been in here."

She smiled. "Markos videoed everything for me. It feels like I've been here a million times."

Surely she could be talked out of this. He had to try. "I'm

not sure what you're up to here, Katarina, but there has to be a better way. I don't see how you can sleep at night after killing kids."

"Shut up and do what I'm telling you to do."

He'd hit a nerve. He'd give her a few minutes before he brought it up again.

"Here," she said. She reached into the backpack she carried and handed him a cylinder the size of a thermos. "You'll want to attach this to a nozzle located under here." She pointed to the spot on the line they'd discovered earlier.

"Okay," he said. "But I still don't see why you need me to do it. You seem quite capable of handling this yourself."

"Kovacs try not to get our hands dirty," she said with a small smile.

The force of her words hit him. She had no intention of letting him, or Maggie, or Heidi, ever live. His fingerprints would be on the bottle. If it was ever discovered, there would be no proof to point back to her. The Kovacs could even argue that Markos had gone rogue and they'd had no awareness of his intentions.

Sure, the FBI would know they'd been behind it all, but their evidence would be circumstantial. Once the anthrax made it into the bottles and was distributed, the Kovacs would make a fortune from their other holdings, and they'd have gotten away with a perfect crime.

Not that he had any intention of letting it get that far. He'd play along, but if she was going to kill him, he'd go to his grave knowing her plan would ultimately fail.

"Here." She handed him the bottle. "You might want to be careful around that. Maybe hold your breath," she said.

He took the bottle. "The tubing is installed underneath," she said. "We've succeeded in contaminating several shipments with a harmless substance, so we know we've got the pressure right," she said. "It's time to put this baby in action."

Blake slid under the blower. Katarina held a flashlight for him. "There, do you see it?"

He tried to pretend it was the first time he'd ever noticed the contraption. "When did Mark do this?"

"It wasn't too hard. This thing messes up all the time, doesn't it?"

"Yes," he said. She was right. Mark could have done this while he stood five feet away and he wouldn't have noticed. He wouldn't have even been suspicious if he'd seen Mark climb out from under there during or after a run.

"Okay, I've found it," he told her. "What do you want me to do?"

"I believe you should be able to connect the tubing and there should be a place for the bottle to be tucked under where no one will see it."

She was right. Blake went to work. She hovered over him, watching his every move. It only took a few minutes to make the connections. Mark had done a good job. Once the line started, this little system he'd rigged up would shoot a tiny puff of what had to be anthrax into each of the water bottles as they came down the line. As small as the anthrax spores were, they wouldn't be noticeable in the finished product.

"Why us?" He tightened a fitting around the tubing.

Katarina shrugged. "Because you're the best."

"Thanks," he said.

She laughed at his sarcasm.

"This was all my idea. I knew a company like yours would get some interesting accounts. Markos had a legitimate engineering degree. We thought if we could put him in place, we'd be able to perfect the application. We expected to be here a few weeks, but Markos kept messing stuff up. I was ready to bail, but then you landed the ballpark account. It was like a sign."

Blake turned his head to glare at Katarina. "You've put a lot into this."

"Indeed. And I'm not going to let Markos growing a conscience stop us."

"Is that why you killed him?"

Her mouth flattened into two thin lines. "He was an idiot. Every job I gave him, he flubbed. How many times did he try to kill you? He was furious when he learned I'd intervened."

"You intervened?"

"You think he'd have ever hurt your precious sister?" She rolled her eyes. "She's the princess of the family, isn't she? Her death would have had you all in so much turmoil we could have turned the bottles purple and you wouldn't have noticed." She clicked her tongue in disgust. "But she got lucky. You both did. I still haven't figured out how you survived the present I left in your Mountain Dew."

Bragging on Heidi wouldn't do either of them any good. Not now. If Katarina didn't know what Heidi was capable of, he wasn't about to help her out.

"I guess we're hard to kill," he said.

Katarina snorted.

"Didn't you think it would look a little suspicious, killing off all three of us in one weekend?"

Katarina groaned. "Don't blame the stroke on us. We had nothing to do with that. We never wanted the whole family out of commission. We need this place to keep operating. After that weekend, we had to slow things down. Didn't want to draw too much attention to how hazardous it had become to be a Harrison."

She leaned closer. "Let me see what you've done." She didn't touch anything, but she examined it all. She obviously knew how it was supposed to look, and she was checking to be sure he hadn't messed anything up.

Blake knew this line would never run tomorrow, but he

wouldn't take any chances. If Katarina Kovac killed him tonight, fine. But he'd never allow anthrax to be pumped into those bottles.

He'd been waiting for the right opportunity, and when it came, he took it.

Bless Markos.

Katarina, looking around with a flashlight, wouldn't have been able to see the bypass Markos had installed. It made sense. He could leave the anthrax in place, and then toggle the switch to contaminate certain products while leaving others clean. The beauty of it was he'd slid the toggle behind a beam. Blake had missed it when he'd been looking at it earlier today, but he had no doubt about how it worked.

The sense of peace that had descended in the car now flooded over him. No matter what, he would be able to face the next few hours with the certainty that the anthrax would never harm anyone.

"One more thing, Blake," Katarina said. "I need you to pull that protective sleeve off the bottle for me."

"Why?"

"Just do it, please."

"Are you planning to kill me with this stuff?" That would not be a fun way to go.

"Of course not," she said.

He removed the fabric from the bottle and could see why she'd wanted it gone. The bottle was stainless steel and blended in to the equipment. No one would ever notice it.

"Do me a favor and put both hands on it and shake it. I want to be sure it's secure. Don't want you to have left it up there where it will crash to the floor once the system powers up, now, do we?"

Blake grabbed the bottle and gave it a shake. "It's not going anywhere, Katarina."

"Excellent," she said. "Out we go."

She backed out, always keeping the gun pointed at him.

He'd have loved to get it away from her, but there wasn't enough room under the equipment for any big swings.

When he stepped out from the blower, he stumbled. Weird. His hands tingled and his vision blurred.

Katarina gave him a tight smile. "Come on." She pointed to the door. Why were there two doors where there was only supposed to be one? He blinked. Tripped over thin air and went down to one knee.

"Oh, dear," Katarina said. "I may have been a bit aggressive on the dose. You can't pass out yet—you're too heavy to carry. Let's get you to the car."

She slid the gun into her backpack and steered him out to the parking lot. He couldn't stop her. His arms weren't cooperating. She propped him up against the car and opened the back door. The last thing he remembered seeing was the torn fabric near the dome light. The car door slammed. The engine started.

Then nothing.

NINETEEN

"Blake! Blake!" The voice sounded far away. "Come on, wake up. Fight. I need you to wake up." The voice sounded closer. Was someone touching him?

Yes. Hands. On his face. His arm.

"Blake?"

He knew that voice. He tried to respond. "Hei—"

"Thank You, God. Thank You." A weight pressed against his chest. Her head? His arms were slow to obey, but they found their way to the curls spilling all over his shirt. He blinked several times, but everything remained pitch-black. Was he blind?

"I…I can't…I can't see you," he said.

Her hands caressed his face. "It's okay," she said. "I can't see you, either. There's a light socket in the middle of the room but no bulb. I found switches, but they don't turn anything on or off. I caught a flash of light when Katarina brought you in, but as soon as she closed the door, nothing."

The events of the past few hours were pinging around in his mind. "Maggie?"

"Asleep," Heidi said. "She's amazing. So brave. She's done everything I asked her to do, although I have a sneaking suspicion Katarina laced her food with a sleeping pill because she fell asleep fast and has stayed that way."

"What happened?"

Heidi told him everything, from her conversation with Maggie to the moment she'd lost consciousness. "I was out for at least two hours. Maggie said she rolled me in here in a wheelbarrow and dumped me on the floor."

"Ouch."

"Yeah, well she didn't even bother to dump you," she said. A metallic sound reverberated through the space. "She wheeled you in and left before I had an opportunity to do anything to get us out of here."

Frustration etched her words, "I've made a thorough search," she said. "The walls are paneling. I managed to pull a piece away, but there's cement block behind it. No windows. As best as I can tell, the ceiling is Sheetrock with one light socket."

"Sounds like you've been busy." He tried to sit up. "I don't understand why we're here."

Heidi didn't answer.

"Do you know?"

"I have a guess."

"Let's hear it."

"You first," she said. "Tell me what happened after we were taken."

Blake filled her in, choosing his words with care in case Katarina was listening. He didn't mention the switch. He'd rather have Heidi believe he'd set off an anthrax scare than have Katarina run back to the plant and flip the switch.

Heidi slid her hand into his. "Then that confirms it," she said.

He already knew, but he couldn't stop himself from asking. "Confirms what?"

"She plans to kill us."

"I was afraid you were going to say that."

They sat in silence for a while. Blake's mind continued to clear and he flexed his arms and legs. Maggie lay beside him and he planted light kisses on her face, thankful she was alive and oddly relieved that she was sleeping through the ordeal.

"Might help work the drug out of your system if you walk around," Heidi said. "Run your hands along the walls. And be sure to dodge the wheelbarrow."

He measured off the room with his steps. He'd guess it was twelve by twelve feet. The ceiling was low. Maybe eight feet. If he jumped, he could touch it.

He found Heidi and Maggie again and sat beside them. "Do you have a plan?"

"I've got several. They're all terrible." She laughed and he appreciated her attempt at humor.

"Will they come looking for you?" he asked, whispering in her ear.

"Yes," she said. "If my original plan had worked, they would have tracked us by now."

"How?"

"Maggie's bow."

"Her what?"

"You gave me permission to track her," she said. "Months ago."

"I know, but I didn't know you'd put a tracker in her hair bow."

"We put one in every single hair accessory she has," Heidi said. "Well, I didn't. One of the agents did."

"So where's the cavalry?"

"The bow she's wearing is new. Her grandmother bought it for her this morning."

"Oh."

"Yeah. And since you haven't heard from Max, that means no one was looking for me yet when Katarina contacted you."

"What makes you say that?"

"If Max couldn't reach me, you would be the next person he would call."

Blake reached for his phone but his pocket was empty.

"Don't bother. I already checked. She must have taken your phone after you passed out."

"When will Max get worried?"

Heidi cleared her throat. "Probably not for a while. Not tonight anyway."

"What's special about tonight?"

Heidi didn't answer right away. "Max has been trying to give us some time alone. He told me he was going to make himself scarce," she said in a low voice. Blake knew that if he could see her face, it would glow with embarrassment.

"I have a standing check-in at 10:00 p.m. No matter where I am or what I'm doing. I send three text messages. One to him, one to Uncle Frank, one to Sara. If everything is okay, I send them a group text with nothing more than good-night. If everything is not okay but I still have my phone, I tell them I love them. If I don't text at all, I get phone calls. If I don't answer, Max will track my phone. Which he will discover is either in the creek where Katarina made me drop it, or offline if it didn't survive the water."

"Then what?"

"They'll try to track us. They'll go to the house first, then the plant. They'll find your car, but then it gets tricky. I don't want to give you false hope. I don't know where we are. Maggie doesn't know where we are. All I know is we aren't far from the plant. Fifteen to thirty minutes at the most, and Maggie said the road was bumpy and windy, so I'm guessing we are in a cabin off an old logging road."

"There's only about a hundred of those around."

"When they find your car, they'll know something is wrong, and —" she dropped her voice to a whisper " — I think we can be confident that plant operations will be suspended until we are found."

"But you aren't confident they will find us in time."

"No. I'm sorry, but I'm not."

Katarina's voice reached them through the thick walls. She was yelling at someone. Blake strained to hear her. Heidi stood and repositioned the wheelbarrow in front of them like a shield.

The yelling grew louder and then ended.

"I'd like to hear your horrible plans, if it's all the same to you," he whispered to Heidi.

"I've got a tiny knife she didn't discover when she searched me," she said. "You're tall enough to stand on the wheelbarrow and try to cut through the ceiling where the light fixture is. As far as I can tell, it's the only weak spot in this place. If we could get a big enough hole in the ceiling, I could get up there and catch her by surprise."

"You're right. That's a horrible plan."

"It's the best I've got. Do you have a better one?"

He loved how she asked. No rancor or animosity. No challenge. She actually thought he might have a better idea.

He wished he did.

"I've got nothing, but then, my brain is still scrambled. What did she do to me?"

"Probably the same thing she did to me. It's a paralytic absorbed through the skin. It's powerful but not long-lasting. Keep moving around. It will help. Water would be a good idea and she brought some in here, but after Maggie fell asleep, I was afraid to touch it or any of the food."

The door rattled and Blake stepped in front of Heidi and Maggie. "I'm afraid this is where I leave you," Katarina said. "I need you to know, this isn't how I wanted things to end."

A door slammed.

The silence that followed was broken when Heidi pounded on the door. The knob rattled as she tried to yank it from the door. "Let me help," he said. Together, they pulled and twisted. They kicked at the door, rammed their shoulders into it. It wouldn't budge.

Heidi used her knife on the screws. It took forever in the dark, but eventually, she got the knob loose enough that they were able to pull it from the door. Blake looked through the opening. A faint light flickered in through a window he could see about fifteen feet away, but it didn't illuminate the room they were in at all.

"She must have braced the door somehow," he said.

"I think you're right."

He turned to her, pulling her close, running his hands through her hair, then kissing her face. "I love you," he said. "I know it's a little late to be mentioning it, but it's true. I love you and I want to be with you forever. I'll sell my share of the business and move to DC if that's what you want. I know you're probably thinking it's easy for me to say that since we are about to die, but I mean it. I've been thinking about it for a while. I don't ever want to be apart from you."

Heidi's hand covered his lips. "I love you, too," she said and pressed her lips to his. "When we get out of this, we can talk about it more. There's an FBI resident agency in Asheville. I've heard they're hiring…"

He kissed her again. "You think we can figure this out?"

"I know we can," she said. "First, we have to figure out how to get out of here."

"Then hand me your knife and point me toward this light fixture."

Blake pulled the wheelbarrow over and stood on it. Heidi's hand wrapped around his and she placed the rubber handle of the knife in his palm.

Blake found the housing for the light and began cutting away at the Sheetrock. Once he got a decent opening, he returned the knife to Heidi and pulled at the Sheetrock with his hands. Dust flew in his eyes.

"Hang on," Heidi said as a piece fell to the floor. "Let me slide Maggie over."

With Maggie out of the way, he continued to rip at the Sheetrock, using the knife when necessary.

His arms shook with exertion, but he had managed to open up a space a few feet wide. The problem was he couldn't tell if there was any open space above or if there was another floor.

"Put me on your shoulders and let me see what I can feel," Heidi said. She scrambled up and they both had to duck to keep her from hitting her head on the ceiling. Once back under the hole, her body shifted as she inspected the opening.

"It's…almost…big enough," she said, straining with each word. "I can't see anything, but it feels cooler. My guess is that I'd be in the rafters. If I can get up here, maybe I'll be able to see some stars or something that will give us a little light."

She climbed back down and he went to work on the hole with new vigor. He'd been at it two or three minutes when Heidi's hand on his leg made him pause.

"What is it?"

"Do you smell that?"

He sniffed the air. Maybe? He sniffed again.

Heidi's grip on his leg tightened. "Smoke. I smell smoke," she said. Fear permeated her words. He sniffed again.

Yes. Smoke.

He peaked through the doorknob. The room was awash with flame. Katarina Kovac was going to burn them alive.

TWENTY

When Blake stepped aside, Heidi peered through the knob. No! The room on the other side of their prison gleamed with firelight. With the cement walls surrounding them, they would probably die of smoke inhalation before the flames came through the ceiling to claim their bodies. It was a very small comfort.

Heidi fought the tremors coursing through her. Proximity to open fire always triggered a panic attack. *Help me*, she prayed. She could not panic. Not now.

"Blake, get me up there," she said.

Blake put his arms around her. "No. I'll do it," he said.

"The hole isn't big enough and I won't be able to lift you up there," she said. "I've got to do it."

"But the fire! Heidi, the ceiling could crash in at any time. I don't know if I can let you—"

"We have to try," she said. "I'll go through the ceiling and down into the other room and see if I can get the door open. You'll have to be ready to run with Maggie."

The flames in the other room allowed light to seep into their prison from the hole in the ceiling and through the door. Not much light, but enough that she could see through his expressions the battle raging in Blake's mind.

"You have to let me do this, Blake."

She saw the moment when he accepted it was the only

way. He pulled her into a fierce embrace. One quick kiss. One whispered "Hurry." Then she clambered onto his shoulders and into the tight space between the rafters.

The heat smacked her face and her body trembled. Every cell in her being wanted to escape the flames, but she forced herself to keep moving forward. The rafters had warmed, but weren't too hot to touch yet. She crawled, one hand on one rafter, one knee on another, and made her way past the cement walls. Once through, she sat on the rafter and kicked at the ceiling, over and over. Smoke had filled the attic space making each breath a commodity with a rapidly dwindling supply.

Finally, her foot broke through. "Yes!"

The heat engulfing her foot caused her to yank it back into the attic. Flames followed. Frantic, she went back to kicking the edges of the opening. Pieces fell to the floor below and more smoke billowed around her.

With one final heave, a huge piece of Sheetrock crashed. Heidi reached for the rafter with her hands, intending to use it to swing herself below. Her hands jerked back of their own accord as flames licked the freshly exposed fuel.

Father, help me, she prayed again and again. She had to get down there. Into the flames. Or they were all dead. But jumping into that inferno would probably kill her. Images of Blake and Maggie filled her mind. She focused on the memories of their smiles and their laughter and their love. With one final prayer that God would help them move on, she jumped.

She landed hard, but managed to avoid catching on fire. If she could get them out…

"Heidi! Heidi! Are you okay?" Blake's calls helped her find the way to the barricaded door.

Katarina hadn't been playing around. Three four-by-four blocks fit snugly at various points along the doorframe.

Four-by-four blocks that smoked as they threatened to burst into flame. She knocked them away, one by one.

Would flames engulf them the moment the door opened and gave the fire a fresh supply of oxygen?

"Blake, get Maggie. Hold her as low to the ground as you can. When I open the door, run straight ahead. I'll try to get to the door ahead of you."

"Okay," Blake said. "I'm ready."

Heidi yanked the door open, then turned and ran for the door to the house. A wall of flame blocked it. She forced herself to run into it and threw the door open as Blake approached. He dove through and hit the porch, rolling Maggie and himself over and over on the ground. Heidi jumped to follow as a piece of ceiling crashed to the floor, burying her in its flames.

The pain woke her. Even before her eyes responded to her repeated command to open, the sounds and smells prepared her for what she would see. A hospital bed. An IV pole. An oxygen mask.

Panic fluttered on the edge of her mind.

Her eyes flew open and she tried to sit up.

"Hey," Blake said. "Where do you think you're going?"

The panic dissipated. He was here. They'd made it out. She tried to smile, but her face didn't cooperate.

"You have a busted lip from where the ceiling collapsed, babe."

Babe. Heidi didn't try to move again for a while. He'd called her babe. He was here. Alive. "Maggie?"

"Completely fine. Singed her eyebrows off, but no permanent damage."

"Where is she? You should be with her. She's going to need—"

"Honey, she's in a bed asleep on the other side of that curtain." He pointed behind his head. "And I know she'll need a lot of help processing what's happened. I'm going to rely on you to help me with that."

Could she help? Maybe as a case study for how *not* to handle trauma. "I don't want her to be like me," she said.

Blake pursed his lips. "I hope she's exactly like you. I hope she's tough and strong and courageous."

"That's not what I meant. I don't want her to live afraid. Or angry."

"She won't, honey. Not with you to help her understand and process everything. Sara came to talk to her yesterday. She thinks she'll make a quick and full recovery."

"Sara's been here? What day is it?"

"Monday, um, no, Tuesday morning. A little after midnight. I've got a special FBI pass that says I can stay with you. The nurse isn't impressed."

She'd been out twenty-four hours. How badly was she injured?

"Hey." Blake leaned closer. "It's okay. You have three broken ribs and a concussion. They flew you out in a chopper. The biggest worry was the smoke inhalation, but you've been breathing on your own with no problems. You've got a few first-degree burns on your back and legs and arms. Your hands have some second-degree burns, but the doctor says they will heal nicely. You've woken up a few times, but my guess is you don't remember."

No, she didn't.

"How did I get out?"

The last thing she remembered was the ceiling crashing and the heat.

He gulped and took a deep breath. "I got Maggie away and went back in after you."

"You came after me?"

"Of course," he said.

"Are you okay?"

"I'm fine. A few minor burns, smoke inhalation. No big deal."

No big deal. This man had walked through fire for her. There was no bigger deal.

She wanted to keep looking at him, keep talking to him, keep convincing herself they'd made it out alive. But the longer she tried to stay awake, the worse she felt. This wretched combination of painkillers and pain was one she knew far too well. "What do they have me on?" She lifted the IV tubing.

"Morphine."

She tried to find a way to turn off the flow.

"Hey!" Blake reached for her hand. "Stop it. You'll be in agony."

"I need to be able to think."

"Honey," Blake said. "You need to be able to heal. There's no rush."

Heidi wanted to argue with him. Something flirted around the edge of her memory, something she needed to do? Or something that was going to happen? It was there, she couldn't quite— Oh! "Katarina?"

"They caught her trying to catch a flight in Charlotte. She lawyered up, but Max says the evidence is overwhelming, especially with three eyewitnesses. And even the Kovacs will have a hard time finding a jury that will let off someone who tried to kill a little girl."

"The anthrax?"

"Secured in some top-secret FBI facility. Our lines are being decontaminated as we speak, and I've been vaccinated and will be enjoying a sixty-day course of antibiotics to be sure I don't get it, since I did handle a bottle of the stuff. No one seems too worried."

"So it's over?"

"It's over. Rest," Blake said.

"Make them lower the dose," she said as she fell back onto her pillow.

When she woke again, Blake sat in the same spot. The only light in the room came from an LED strip under a cabinet.

"You're still here."

At her words, he stood and leaned toward her. The kiss he planted on her forehead couldn't have been more chaste. The effect on her was anything but. She wanted him to kiss her the way he had…how many nights ago?

The look on his face told her he wanted that, too. "I love you, Heidi Zimmerman."

"I love you, too."

He rested his cheek against her forehead for a second, then pulled back a few inches. His Adam's apple bobbed. "I don't know how this will all work out, but it doesn't matter anymore. I meant what I said before. I'll sell my shares and move to DC."

"You don't have to—"

"All I need to know is that you're coming home to me. Maggie adores you, and she'll be far better off to have you in her life than she would be if she had to say goodbye because I'm too stubborn to pick up and move."

Heidi couldn't stop the tears rolling down her cheeks. "Blake," she said. "I don't want you to move to DC."

Hurt and confusion etched his features and she hurried to explain.

"I want to stay here. I wasn't kidding about the Asheville office. I'm sure I can wrangle a transfer of some kind."

"I don't know. Aren't you the Kovac family expert? Doesn't seem like you could do that from here. I don't want you to have to give up your job."

"It will be fine," she said. "I don't see it as giving anything up."

He ran a finger across her cheek. "There is only one thing I want you to give up for me," he said.

"What's that?"

"Your last name."

"You like the name Heidi Harrison, do you?"

"No," Blake said as he leaned in for a kiss. "I love the name Heidi Harrison." His lips pressed against hers. "Don't you?"

"I do."

* * * * *

Dear Reader,

I'm thrilled that you joined Heidi and Blake on their journey to find justice and love. I often find myself writing about God's sovereignty and wisdom, as well as His forgiveness and grace, probably because I frequently find myself struggling to rest in His plan for my life and I always need more grace!

His plan for this book was nothing I could have dreamed up on my own, and I have a pretty good imagination! *Covert Justice* is my first published novel and I wrote most of it during The Search for a Killer Voice contest the Love Inspired Suspense editors hosted in the spring of 2014.

I entered the contest even though I hadn't finished writing the book and didn't know exactly how it would end! As a busy mom of three young children, I had no idea how I would find the time to finish the story, but every time I made it into the next round of the contest God increased my time and my creativity. He always makes a way!

Covert Justice is tangible evidence of God's wisdom, sovereignty, strength and power. I will never be able to see it without reflecting on how He held me and guided me through every step of the publication journey.

I'd love to hear your thoughts about Blake and Heidi's story. You can find me at lynnhugginsblackburn.com where you can sign up for my newsletter and receive an exclusive deleted scene from *Covert Justice*.

Grace and peace,

Lynn Huggins Blackburn